SIERRA
SKULLDUGGERY

Other books by Jerry S. Drake:

The Gunfighter's Apprentice

SIERRA SKULLDUGGERY

•

Jerry S. Drake

AVALON BOOKS
NEW YORK

Published by Thomas Bouregy & Co., Inc.
160 Madison Avenue, New York, NY 10016

Library of Congress Cataloging-in-Publication Data

Drake, Jerry S.
  Sierra skullduggery / Jerry S. Drake.
      p.   cm.
  Sequel to The gunfighter's apprentice.
  ISBN 978-0-8034-9900-3 (hardcover : acid-free paper)
  I. Title.

PS3604.R35S54 2008
813'.6—dc22   2007047387

PRINTED IN THE UNITED STATES OF AMERICA
ON ACID-FREE PAPER
BY HADDON CRAFTSMEN, BLOOMSBURG, PENNSYLVANIA

For Ginny, ever beloved.

Chapter One

"There's someone to see you, Tom," the clerk said as the tall and lean trail-dusty man entered the lobby of the small Auburn hotel. "In the saloon there. Like to have a word with you."

Tom Patterson sighed and looked down at his ragged denim jacket, sweat-stained shirt and soiled jeans. "Lordy, I was looking for taking a bath soon as I got in."

"Wouldn't hurt to have a cold drink. Maybe the gent will buy you one."

Tom looked at the café doors that separated the hotel lobby from the adjacent saloon. "Lord knows I try my best to stay outta hard liquor places. The missus, she got me sober and 'spect's me to stay there."

"You could have a beer, that ain't exactly hard stuff."

"Well, maybe one wouldn't hurt," Tom agreed. "Who's the fellow and what did he say he wanted?"

"Didn't say."

Again, Tom looked down at himself. "Well, he'll have to take me as he sees me, dirt and all." He nodded at the room keys hanging on a pegboard behind the clerk. "Which room?"

"Five, I reckon," the clerk said and reached for a key.

"Mind sending up the boy with some hot water for the tub? Maybe thirty minutes?"

"I'll fetch him and get him started."

Tom nodded his thanks, accepted the key and walked through the louvered doors into the saloon. Two men were sipping beer at the bar, a bartender nowhere in sight. At a table sat a man with a thick head of dark hair, a matching mustache and beard, the latter partially covering a furrowed scar on his left cheek. He appeared near an age of forty, large and strongly built, smartly dressed in a dark suit coat and with a silk cravat at his stiff collar.

"Mr. Patterson?" the man asked, rising. He gestured to a chair. "Could you give me a few minutes of your time?"

Something about him, something I don't like.

Tom walked to the table. "I'm Tom Patterson."

"Patrick Mahoney," the man said and gestured to the chair again. "If you would, please."

Tom remained standing. "What's this about?"

"Can I buy you a drink?"

"What's this about?"

"Very well." Mahoney resumed his seat and looked up at Tom. "I'd like to offer you a job."

"I've got a job."

"Not much of one. Heavy load hauling, hard work, and not too much pay for fellow your age . . . what, forty-two, forty-three?" He shook his head. "Pretty poor pickings for a man of your background and capability."

Tom didn't respond.

"Well, if that suits you, that's just fine," Mahoney said. "What I have in mind for you would only take a week or two, maybe a bit more . . . and the pay will be handsome."

"Handsome?"

"To be negotiated. Do I have your interest?"

"I ain't interested."

"Big money, my friend."

"Not interested."

"Really big money."

"I like my life now. I don't hire out my gun if that's your idea."

Mahoney nodded. "Yes, that is exactly what I have in mind." He gestured to Tom's belt. "I see you're not carrying."

Tom turned away.

"You'd better listen, Mr. Patterson," Mahoney said sharply.

Tom turned back and leaned on the table, looking down into the man's face. "If you know anything about me, you'll not take that tone with me."

Mahoney chuckled. "You may think you've changed, Patterson, but you just showed me who you *really* are."

"I'd not push it."

"I am a stubborn man. And I *do* insist on hiring your gun. After you know the details, you'll actually thank me. You'll thank me for giving you a chance to even an old score and getting paid for it as well."

"Keep your details and your money to yourself. Whatever you think about me settling some damned score, I ain't interested. I *don't* hire out my gun."

"You so well off that money's not welcome?"

"I'm going upstairs and when I come down, I don't want to see you."

"If settling a score won't do it or money won't buy you, I *did* come prepared."

Tom waited.

"You've got a very pretty wife—"

Tom's hands flashed across the table and grasped the lapels of the man's coat. He dragged Mahoney over the table and slammed him to the floor, kicked him in the stomach, then placed his boot on the man's throat and leaned over him. "What were you saying about my wife?"

It took a few seconds for the man to force out a pained response. "Anything happens to me, something happens to her."

Tom jammed his boot heel down. "You want somebody killed? You're just about ready to have that happen."

"She's already in our hands," the man wheezed, "and you're covered."

Tom looked up and found the two men at the bar with guns trained on him.

"Let me up," Mahoney croaked.

Tom stepped back and watched as Mahoney used a chair to leverage himself erect. He rubbed his throat and walked to join the two gunmen.

"Your wife is all right, nothing has happened to her," Mahoney said, his voice ragged and whispery. "Nothing will happen to her as long as you behave yourself."

Tom spoke to the two gunmen. "You gents are taking a chance carrying weapons here in this town. Law don't like that."

"You don't have a side arm," Mahoney said as he rubbed his throat. "Probably a mistake."

Tom settled slowly into a chair. "You wanted to talk, let's talk."

"The money offer is still good," Mahoney said although he remained standing.

Casually, Tom folded his hands across his chest. "What's this about my wife?"

"Insurance, Mr. Patterson. She won't be harmed. We've taken her to a place where she'll be comfortable. She'll be treated with courtesy and respect. Soon as your job is over, she'll be released and you'll both be well rewarded for your work and her inconvenience."

Tom's right hand found an itch on his chest, followed

it inside his jacket and flashed out with a small multi-barreled pepperbox pistol.

Surprised and dismayed, the two gunmen stepped back. One started to raise his revolver to fire but hesitated as Tom trained the small weapon at his chest.

"Always carry this little hideout just in case." He waved the weapon. "I can probably get the two of you even if you finish me. Is he paying you enough to take the chance?"

Mahoney raised his hand very slowly and waved it at the men. "No need for a showdown. Another time. Just remember that if you do anything to me, your lady will pay the bill. We'll talk again."

He turned his back to Tom and headed for the door and out to the street. The two gunmen, confused and bewildered, backed out behind him.

Tom rose from his chair and walked quickly through the café doors into the hotel lobby and hurried to the window. Across the street he saw Mahoney on the boardwalk talking to the two men. In pantomime it was an angry trio, hands jabbing the air with abrupt gestures. A few seconds later they parted, Mahoney going one way, the pair the other.

"Thought I heard a ruckus in there," the clerk spoke from across the lobby. "Everything okay?"

"Maybe," Tom replied as he slid the pepperbox into his inside jacket pocket.

"You want that room now?"

"Not now. I won't be staying."

"That gentleman you was with?"

Tom turned to face the clerk.

"Seems to me I've seen him once or twice before back when I was living down in Placerville. Something to do with the railroad."

"What do you mean?"

"He, maybe, might work for them," the clerk told him. "You say you ain't staying?"

Tom shook his head. "I'm heading home as soon as I saddle my horse. Should be there 'fore morning."

"Gonna be a dark night, watch where your horse steps," the clerk advised.

Tom nodded. "Older fellow named Willie that's working for me, when he comes in you tell him to bring the rig home as soon as he can. I gotta run."

"Something wrong back home?"

"God willing, I hope not."

With an abrupt nod of farewell, Tom tossed the room key to the clerk, wheeled, and strode out the door.

"Pity those gents," the clerk said aloud to the empty lobby as he turned to return the key to the peg. "They ain't got no notion of what they've started."

Chapter Two

At the third insistent rapping, the door opened and a pretty blond woman stood behind the screen. "What's all the commotion? What do you want?"

"Mrs. Patterson?" A big man stood with the two others behind him. "Mrs. Tom Patterson?"

She nodded.

"Sorry about our hasty manner, ma'am." A second man stepped forward. "It's downright urgent."

"Who are you?"

"I'm Dan Cavanaugh and this here's Earl Hammond." He gestured to the man beside him. "Him and me, we're with the outfit your husband Tom is hauling freight for." He nodded to a man with a shiny badge on his shirt. "This here is Bill Miller. He's a deputy."

The woman's eyes narrowed as she looked at the lawman. "Something's happened?"

The deputy gave a slow nod. "We got a wire that there's been an accident up on the way to Auburn. Wheel came off his wagon and dumped both your Tom and his helper. Wagon load of that rough cut timber fell on 'em."

"How bad?" she asked.

"Young 'un was killed," Miller said, lowering his head. "Your man is banged up pretty bad. These two gents, they've got a buggy here and will take you right to him."

Cavanaugh spoke once again. "Best you pack a bag with some things, ma'am. He's at a doctor's place and you'll be wanting to stay with him."

"How bad is he?" she persisted.

"Leg's broken, maybe some ribs," Cavanaugh said gravely. "We think he's gonna pull through, but it might help a lot if you was there to give him comfort."

"Can I see that telegram?"

Cavanaugh reached for a hip pocket and then took his hand away with an apologetic gesture. "I guess I left it behind, I'm sorry, ma'am."

Betty regarded him for a few moments and then nodded. "I'll be with you in just a few minutes."

"Soon as you're ready, ma'am. He's been calling for you."

The door closed and the men sat in the sun on the porch steps, their eyes fixed on the distant Sierra Nevada Mountains.

"Nice day," the deputy said after a few minutes.

Cavanaugh nodded. "Working out okay. She's gonna be no problem. Pretty damned easy, I'd say."

Hammond spoke. "We don't know these people. Don't take nothing for granted."

Cavanaugh glanced to Hammond, rolled his eyes, and shrugged. "Ain't counting any chickens, no sir. Careful as we go."

The three men sat in silence, each scanning the quiet street and glancing at the front door of the bungalow.

"Lady's sure taking her time," Miller said. "What with her husband hurt, she don't seem much in a hurry."

"Probably packing," the deputy gave his opinion. "And then, maybe, they ain't all that tight with each other."

With their eyes on the front door of the house, they didn't see Betty Patterson as she came around the side of the house.

"Hands up, gents!" she commanded.

The three startled men swiveled their heads, alarmed to see the woman with the Henry rifle raised to her shoulder.

"Get off them steps and lay facedown there on the grass," she told them. "Mr. Deputy, as you call yourself, you make one move to that handgun and that'll be the all to end all."

Not one of the men moved.

Betty fired a shot into the ground at the lawman's

feet. "I won't waste another bullet. Facedown on that grass right now."

The deputy was the first to move. He rose from the steps and knelt to the ground, then sprawled on his belly, his hands by his side.

"Stretch out them hands straight up over your head. Now!"

The deputy extended his hands and looked back over his shoulder. "Look, lady, there's no call—"

"You're not one of our town deputies."

"No, ma'am, but I'm law all right, you betcha."

"Not likely," Betty countered, pointing the rifle barrel to the ground. "Now, you other two."

Hammond and Cavanaugh moved to the ground, knelt and laid flat beside the deputy. Across the street, a door of a neighbor's house opened and a woman took a tentative step out on her porch.

"It's all right, Cora!" Betty shouted. "Would you send that boy of yours down to the marshal's office? Tell him I got three jaspers here for his jail."

"Sure thing, Betty!" the woman called. "You all right?"

"Got a rifle on 'em! I can handle 'em."

"This is going to go bad for you, lady," the lawman said. "I'm an officer—"

"Shut your mouth!" She moved quickly over the deputy, reached down and pulled his revolver from his holster. She backed away and tucked it inside her apron pocket.

"Your husband, Mrs. Patterson," Hammond said. "We came to tell you he was hurt—"

"You think I'm a fool? If something really happened, Bert Stevens down there at our stable would be the very first one to come tell me, not three strangers I never ever seen before."

Across the street, a small boy came out of the door and hurried to the street, staring.

"Get going, Timmy!" his mother called. "Run fast!"

The boy stared for a moment longer, then raced down the street toward the town center.

"One more thing," Betty said in a scathing voice. "That young fellow, George Martinez, who always rides with Tom on his wagon? He ain't killed, he's got himself married right here at the Methodist Church this very morning."

"We must've misunderstood," Hammond protested. "Whoever it was."

"We'll just find out what's really going on when the town marshal comes here," she said. "Such as he is."

"You need some help?" the neighbor woman called as she hurried across the street to join Betty. A slim, plain-faced woman, she was in her late twenties, a few years younger than Betty. She looked down at the sprawled threesome. "Land sakes, what did they do?"

"Nothing yet, but I think they was planning something. Wanted me to go with them."

"Go with them? Where?"

"Some cock-and-bull story about Tom getting hurt."

The woman fixed Betty with a questioning stare. "How do you know he ain't?"

"Things they said just didn't sound right. And, down deep, something told me Tom was just fine."

The woman nodded. "I know that feeling. Women can sense when trouble comes to a loved one." She looked down at the men again. "Anything I can do to help?"

Betty took the revolver from her apron. "Know how to use this?"

The woman took the gun and nodded. "Did a little target shooting with my brothers on our place back there in Kaintuck."

Other neighbor women and a couple of old men came from their houses and stood outside the picket fence. Cora walked over to them and explained what was happening.

"Here's Timmy coming back," Betty called to her neighbor. "Nobody with him."

The youngster's run slowed to a hesitant walk, head bowed as he walked to his mother. "Ain't nobody who could come," he said in a quiet way yet audible to all. "Just the jailer guy and he said he couldn't come."

"That's all right, Timmy," Betty called. "Guess we can take care of 'em ourselves." She poked the muzzle of the Henry into the cheek of Hammond's rump. "Get up, we're going to take us a little walk down to the jail."

"What about my horse?" the burly deputy said, raising himself up on one arm.

"Somebody will fetch your horses and your buggy," she responded. "Now up on your feet with your hands reaching high."

Slowly the men rose from the lawn, hands high above their heads. With Betty and Cora behind them, they started the walk toward the town square. A cluster of neighbors trailed behind them. As the procession moved into the business area, men came out of the stores and watched the small parade.

"Whatcha got there, young lady?" a man called from the side of the street.

"Maybe it's Jesse and his gang!" came another voice.

"Naw, can't be them," corrected a man coming from the barbershop, lather on his face and a cloth around his neck. "Jesse's bunch got shot up at Northfield three, four years back."

"That's a fact, but some say he's riding again," the barber added. "Be that so, they sure ain't any of Jesse's gang."

"You men ought to be ashamed!" came a call from an old man at the dry goods store. "Letting women-folk get the drop on you!"

The procession gathered new followers, men and boys falling in as they crossed the square, and then the gathering fanned out in a crescent as Betty and Cora came to the front of the jail.

"Would one of you knock on the door and ask that man inside to let us in?" Betty said to the small crowd.

"Glad to, ma'am," a middle-aged man said and moved to the jail door and rapped on it. "What'd they do?"

"We ain't done nothing!" Hammond protested. "She's crazy."

"They was up to no good," Betty said cryptically. "That's as far as I got a need to say."

The door opened and a slender, elderly man with a wreath of white hair stepped out and blinked in the sunshine. "What's going on?"

"Put these no accounts in your jail, if you would, please," Betty said.

"What did they do?"

"I think they was planning a kidnapping."

"Who?"

"Me."

The old man considered for several seconds. "The marshal ain't here. His deputy neither."

"When will he be back?"

The old man shrugged. "Might be a spell."

"I can't stand out here with a gun on 'em all day," Betty told him. "What do you want to do?"

The old man took a long time before answering. "Take 'em on in, I guess." He stepped back out of the doorway.

"You heard him, gents," she addressed the three men. "Move on."

In single file, Miller, Hammond and Cavanaugh walked through the door with Betty and Cora following.

Cora closed the outer door to shut out the townspeople as the jailer unlocked an inner door to the cells beyond.

"Don't know that I ought to be doing this without the marshal's okay," the old man grumbled. "We'll put 'em in that back cell there."

The jailer locked the protesting men in the cell and returned to the outer office. "You gonna stick around and press charges?"

"I got some things to do first," she said. "I'll go over to the telegraph office and send to that Auburn hotel where my husband always stays. Then, after I check with Bert at the stable, I'm going out to the sawmill and see if they've heard anything."

"You need a ride, Betty?" Cora asked. "My buggy's hitched. I was fixing to go to the store. I could carry you to the mill."

"I'll take my own, Cora, but I do appreciate the offer. I might be a spell."

"Anything I can do to help, you just call."

Outside, the crowd had dispersed and the two women along with young Timmy crossed the square and walked the street to their homes. Cora waved her good-bye and Betty headed for the small barn behind her house. She opened the door and walked inside. She moved to one of the two stalls and lifted the bar. She stepped in and patted her mare on the nose and smiled as the horse nuzzled her hand, then her shoulder. "He's all right, Missy," she said softly. "He ain't no man to ever get killed by some damned accident." Nonetheless, tears came as she led the horse out of the stall toward the buggy in the center aisle.

Chapter Three

A little before sunrise, Tom tied the reins of his lathered horse to the hitching rail, noting the lamplight in the front room of his house. Weary and worried, he hurried up the steps and through the porch and front door.

Betty roused from her doze in a chair, startled by the abrupt intrusion and then came to her feet with a cry of joy. "Tom, thank God!"

"Bett, are you all right?" Tom took her into his arms and pulled her tight against him.

"I'm fine, I'm fine," she spoke against his chest. "They said you were hurt."

"I ain't hurt," he assured her.

She shook her head. "You get my telegraph?"

He laughed. "Must've come after I left." His voice changed to concern. "They said you was taken!"

She pulled away to look up into his face and nodded. "They surely tried." She made a face. "What's going on, Tom? There's something crazy happening."

They sat holding each other for a long time while the early morning sun streamed through the windows and brightened the living room. Betty told her story first and Tom followed with his.

Afterward, Tom led his horse to the backyard barn for a rubdown, water and feed while Betty fixed breakfast.

"What do you make of it?" she asked as Tom poured coffee into a mug and sat at the table.

"Damned if I know," he replied, sipping the steaming brew with care.

They sat silently through pancakes and bacon, each with their own thoughts.

Betty cleared the table and washed the dishes. Finished, she turned to her husband. "Those men at the jail. Soon as I freshen up and get dressed, let's go ask them."

"You let 'em go?" Tom shouted.

Marshal Judd was a fat man with a breathing problem just short of consumption. He sat behind his wooden desk in his extra large bib overalls and lowered his real chin into the fold of two others. His eyes peered out of his half-closed lids, then glanced with significant meaning toward the door to the cells. "We held 'em for a while, but we had other troublemakers to deal with," he wheezed. "We only got us two cells back there and we needed 'em both."

"Why did you let them go?" Tom persisted.

"Couldn't see why not," the marshal replied and turned to Betty. "No offense, ma'am, but they said you got all excited about nothing. They was just asking for information about something that happened back there when you all lived in Colorado. Said you got the wrong idea."

"That's lying talk," Betty declared. "What they had in mind—"

"The deputy confirmed their story, ma'am, and—"

"You don't butt in when my wife is talking and you ain't going to question what she says."

The marshal grunted what appeared to be some sort of an apology.

"From what my husband tells me," Betty said evenly, "they had some scheming thing to hold me prisoner while some others up in Auburn made him do something bad."

"Such as, ma'am?"

"I think it had to do with some killing," Tom interposed.

"Killing who?"

Tom shrugged. "That just never was said."

The heavy man studied the top of his bare desk. "Well, I might've held onto 'em had I known any of this. Way it was, the deputy showed some identifying that he was for real a lawman."

"What kind of identifying?" Tom asked.

"Well, his badge."

"Said his name was Bill Miller," Betty said.

The marshal gave her a questioning look.

"Ain't that what he told you?" Betty asked. "Him and the other two, Hammond and Cavanaugh?"

The marshal heaved back in his chair and opened the belly drawer of the desk. He fished out a slip of paper and regarded it gravely. "Deputy's name was . . . Bob Jones." He paused and cleared his throat. "There was Clyde Brown and the other one, Jim . . ." He paused with a stricken look.

"Smith?" Tom ventured.

The marshal gave a slow, embarrassed nod.

"Jones, Smith and Brown," Tom mused. "Who took down them names?"

The marshal glanced at the door to the cells. "Old Luke took 'em. That ain't no excuse for me, but I just didn't put no mind to it 'til I just now saw 'em wrote down. Seemed okay when I was talking to 'em one by one."

Tom sighed and turned to Betty. "No use to go no farther. Let's get home."

They left the jail and climbed into their buggy, Tom handling the reins, clucking Missy forward.

"Who did they want you to kill?" Betty asked.

"We never quite got around to that," Tom responded.

"Why not?"

"Well, they had guns on me and I had a mighty poor one on them. Didn't seem the time to do much more talking."

"Does it bother you? Knowing that somebody, somewhere, is going to be killed?"

Tom nodded slowly. "Been thinking on that. Bothers me a sight more why they wanted me."

Betty waited.

"Seems like with all the bad men in California who'd have done the job, why me?" He snapped the rein ends over Missy's rump and hurried the horse to a trot.

"Why me?" Tom repeated for the fourth time that night as he pulled his nightshirt down over his head.

"Because of what you used to do, I reckon," Betty said from her side of the bed, tired of the subject. "Maybe, for now, we can just put it out of our minds."

Tom nodded as he turned down the lamp and slipped under the covers. In the dark, he really couldn't dismiss his thoughts. With his marriage to Betty and their move to California from Colorado, he had thought gunplay was a thing of the past. His checkered gunfighting career, involving violence on both sides of the law, had climaxed in the mining town of Gold Stream in the Rocky Mountains. Hired for a goodly price to teach gun-handling skills to an outlaw-threatened young man, he and his apprentice had fought and routed the notorious Jack Moss and his gang.

Seeking a new and peaceful life, with enough money for a new and sensible life, they had settled in the small, burgeoning California settlement of Red Cliff northeast of Sacramento. For a reasonable down payment,

Tom bought an established drayage business from Bert Stevens, the retiring owner. A steady demand for freight hauling between his base in Red Cliff and other California communities brought money enough to make the payments on the remaining debt, to pay the stable rent and to provide a decent income as well. With his long, sturdy wagon and a team of Belgian draft horses, he was never without work and he highly prized such independence.

"Left Uncle Willie up there in Auburn with the rig," he said in the dark. "I sure hoped he'd have the sense enough to find and bring back a load instead of deadheading back like he did."

"Get some sleep, Tom."

"Had to leave her there to get home to see how you were."

"I'm fine."

"We need to go over to the state cap."

Betty raised her head and turned to her husband. "To Sacramento?"

"Yep."

"You hate that place."

"Maybe so, but I got a notion it's where I might find some answers."

"About what happened?"

"Yep."

"Nothing happened to you or me. We'd just best let it go and don't worry it no more."

"It's worrying me and I think I know where I can find some unworrying."

"That ain't no word."

"Now it is."

She buried her head in her pillow and muttered something unintelligible.

"You could come along and do some shopping."

"While you're doing what?"

"Talking with them railroad people."

Again, her head came up. "Railroad people? What do they have to do with anything?"

"It ain't much of a clue, but them folks just might be the ones to give us some answers. Clerk told me that Mahoney fellow might have been working for them."

She sighed. "You're not going to forget about it, are you?"

"Get some shut-eye, hon," he told her with a yawn. "We'll talk about it in the morning."

Chapter Four

They sat in the narrow reception area of the railroad's legal office. The room was spare with neither paintings nor accessories although a thick Persian rug woven with many muted colors graced the polished wooden floor. The walls featured dark mahogany wood panels that stretched to the high caramel-colored ceiling. Two tall, narrow windows in the outside wall admitted thin shafts of intense sunlight that emphasized the gloom rather than relieving it. In one blazing beam of light, a middle-aged male secretary sat at a large mahogany desk, his eyes studiously focused on papers before him. Once in awhile, as he transferred a sheet from one neat pile to another, he looked up and scowled.

"I got a notion to bust him," Tom whispered. "We been waiting, what? Two hours?"

Betty nodded. "That's why I came along. To keep you from busting someone."

"You look nice," he told her.

She smiled her appreciation and looked down at her clothing. It was her best, a proper dress not at all like the revealing ones she had worn while working at the Gold Strike saloon back in Colorado. It was a light gray muslin with a long skirt, a form-fitted bodice, a high collar, and pearl buttons. Tom, in contrast, had settled for a clean blue shirt, fairly new jeans, and his best broad-brimmed western hat now held in his hand.

"I ain't here to be admired," he said as her eyes regarded him. "I'm here to ask some questions."

Across the room, the secretary rose from his desk and walked down a hallway. After a few minutes, he reappeared. "Mr. Sherwood will see you now."

Tom and Betty rose from their chairs and walked to the hallway. The secretary gave a slight nod to them, turned, and led them down the corridor. Near the end of the hallway, he paused at an ornately carved walnut door and gave it three soft raps.

"Come in!" came a muted male voice.

The secretary opened the door and stood aside to usher Betty then Tom into the office. He gave another nod and closed the door as he left.

The private office was spacious and well appointed. At one end, a slight, silver-haired man in a severe black suit was dwarfed at his huge desk, a wall of leather-bound legal volumes behind him. At the opposite end of the room, there was a small conference table with six leather chairs in the sunlight of a floor to ceiling window. On a sidewall, there were dramatic paintings of large steam locomotives traversing snowy mountain passes, passenger trains speeding along picturesque California seascapes, and a colorful canvas depicting a prairie train being pursued by Indians on horseback. On the opposite wall, a huge map of the western United States was webbed with colored lines representing railroad routes.

The slight pallid-faced man at the desk, like his subordinate of the outer office, seemed totally absorbed in the legal papers on his desk. Either because of his intense concentration or a deliberate disregard, he didn't look up to Tom and Betty. He continued to study the legal briefs, occasionally raising a pince-nez to his eyes to examine a document closely.

Finally, he removed the reading glasses, raised his head and regarded his visitors with a dour expression. "Take a seat at the table," he said with a nuance of disdain. "I'll be with you in a minute."

Tom escorted Betty to the table and pulled back a chair for her, then seated himself. Side by side, they looked out the window at the bustling street three stories below. There were streams of commercial wagons and personal buggies moving in opposite directions, many pedestrians walking on the sidewalks. In the distance, over the low buildings, they could see the Central Pacific railyards with puffing switch engines moving freight cars to different sidings.

Mr. Sherwood rose from his desk and walked toward them. He was a short man, not much over five feet in height. An expertly tailored suit still could not conceal a potbelly that contradicted his slender frame. He paused beside the couple and gave an unsmiling nod to Betty, then another to Tom. "Langdon Sherwood," he introduced himself, "Mr. and Mrs. Patterson?" He moved immediately to the chair at the head of the table and seated himself. "You have a problem that you claim involves the railroad?"

Tom cleared his throat. "Not exactly. What I said downstairs has to do with some fellow who *might* work for the railroad. I was hoping you'd be able to give us some answers."

"Tell me about it."

Tom and Betty spoke, weaving their individual stories into a comprehensive account of attempted abduction and an intended killing.

When they'd finished, Sherwood drummed his fingers on the table. "This is terrible, absolutely terrible. The man at the saloon . . . now, what was his name again?"

"Patrick Mahoney was the name he gave me," Tom said. "A fellow told me he had seen him sometimes down there in Placerville."

Sherwood frowned and shook his head. "Mahoney. Not one of our employees."

"Maybe by another name?"

Again, the small man shook his head. "Not from your description."

"You have a big outfit," Tom persisted. "How can you be sure?"

"Point taken," the lawyer acknowledged. "Of course, we will check into it and I assure you our corporation is in no way involved in any such reprehensible actions."

"How about these other men?" Betty asked. She handed a sheet of paper to Sherwood. "Know any of them?"

Again, he raised the small reading glasses to the bridge of his nose and peered at the note. "You said they used different names?"

Betty nodded. "There are the ones they first gave and then, the ones they said at the jail."

Sherwood shook his head, lowered the glasses and held up the note. "May I keep this?"

Betty nodded.

The lawyer rose and stepped away from the table; his action signaling the interview was over. "Thank you for bringing this to our attention. We'll look into it although I'm sure it really is not in any way related to our corporation."

Tom and Betty rose and started toward the doorway as Sherwood walked ahead of them. Tom paused to look at the colors of lines on the wall map. "These here all your routes?"

The small man took a step back to join him at the map. "Yes, current, proposed and a few out of service."

"I was noticing some of these don't go nowhere."

"Some of the gray lines represent spurs to mines."

"How about those blue ones?"

"Routes either abandoned or postponed."

"Why wouldn't they be finished?"

"Many reasons," the lawyer said, his manner turning brusque. "Difficult terrain, problems in acquiring right of ways . . . a number of concerns."

"This here black one," Tom said as he pointed to one line. "Ends at Placerville?"

"Not very active these days," Sherwood said. "Probably will abandon it in the future if it continues to be unprofitable." He started for the door once again. "I'm sorry, but I have some pressing engagements."

As the elderly operator opened the sliding door, they stepped out of the elevator and Tom looked back with some consternation. "Don't trust that newfangled thing."

Betty smiled. "Did you learn anything?"

"I learned that was one slick snob of a lawyer up there. He says he don't know nothing and, for my money, he ain't ever gonna find out nothing."

"Then why did we come?"

"Only clue I had, that hotel clerk saying that Mahoney might be working for the railroad down around Placerville."

"You think he really does?"

"Maybe not directly, but maybe hires out to 'em."

"You didn't say that to the lawyer."

"He wouldn't have told me."

"*Now* can we forget about it?"

Tom opened the door of the building for Betty to precede him onto the street. "Maybe, maybe not."

Betty looked at him, her eyebrows raised in question.

"Maybe if I did some looking around down there around Placerville, I might find some answers."

"Let's just go on home, Tom. Please."

"Not just yet," Tom said as he took her arm. "Let's go buy you another pretty dress."

Langdon Sherwood stood at the window looking down, watching the man and woman, arm in arm, crossing the busy street. He half-turned, deep thought furrowing his brow. *That fool, Parrish. Has he jeopardized everything with his stupid kidnapping scheme? Perhaps it would be wise to forget about Patterson and proceed without him.*

Although a senior member of the legal department, he knew his position was untenable. Railroads, nowadays, were skittish about land deals and right-of-way acquisitions, worried about the anger and publicity concerning past dubious transactions. He felt no remorse for the hard contracts he had negotiated. People were stupid and deserved to be little rewarded if given anything at all. However, at the end of this month, by his own initiative, he would walk away and leave this railroad's problems to whomever management might choose to replace him.

He returned to his desk and took a notepad from a drawer, reached for a pen, dipped the nib into an open bottle of ink and began to write. In just over a minute, he finished writing, returned the pen to a holder and tore the top sheet from the pad. He walked to his door and hurried to the outer office where his secretary rose, anticipating a directive. "Get in touch with Carl Parrish," Sherwood commanded as he passed the man a note. "Have this telegram sent and delivered to him at this hotel in Virginia City. If we don't hear from him right away, try the hotel in Gold Hill."

He retraced his steps to his office and moved to the window once again and stared down at the bustle of afternoon traffic. He turned around and surveyed his subdued yet splendid office and gave a shrug of mild regret. *When my plan is complete, much more than this will be mine. Unless, something else goes wrong.*

Sherwood willed away any thought of such a calamity with a shake of his head and, with an uncharacteristic smile, returned to finish the work of the day at his desk.

Chapter Five

"You know, you really are a stubborn man," Betty complained. "Sometimes, I don't think you've got a lick of common sense."

"You gonna be all right?"

Betty sighed. "I'll be fine. Go on and do what you got to do and don't worry."

In the early morning, they were standing outside the small barn behind their house, Betty still in her robe. Tom hoisted the saddlebags over the back of Ginger, his chestnut mare and turned to his wife. "Don't know that a woman should be running a business."

"No different than when you're on a delivery. 'Sides, young George is long back from that two-day honeymoon and he and Uncle Willie will help me manage."

She pursed her lips. "I'm just worried that you're sticking your nose where it might get snipped off."

"I won't trust nobody with knives or scissors."

She laughed.

"I won't be but a few days away."

"All because of what that hotel fellow said? That Mr. Sherwood told us he didn't know anything about that man, Mahoney."

"I ain't putting much stock in what some lawyer fellow says. That little jasper seemed more interested in getting a look at us instead of what we was telling him. I don't put no trust in folks in that outfit."

"You just got a mad-on about railroads."

Tom nodded. "Hired on with the Casement brothers not long after the war. Jack and Dan Casement ran that Hell on Wheels train for the Union Pacific and they was hard men."

"Got the job done, I heard," Betty countered.

"Ain't denying that. Damnedest thing you ever saw. Damned train had twenty or more cars. Cars where you'd sleep, cars where you'd eat, blacksmith cars, a carpenter's shop car, flatbed cars carrying the rails." He shook his head with vivid memories. "Them Irishmen was laying nine, ten miles a day across the prairie, lots of days more."

"Now, you sound like you admired railroad people."

"Like you said, they got the job done, but they was sometimes nasty about it. Some of us hired on to keep

Injuns away. A lot of us rebs needed the work, but, then, if there was any complaints from any of the construction gangs about not getting paid or needing medical help when they got hurt, they wanted us to quieten up them that complained."

"Killings?"

Tom took his time to answer. "Well, I heard about it danged near a couple of times and that was enough for me. I lasted a few months and then cut out."

Betty squinted into the slanting rays of the morning sun. "Best you get on your way. Sooner you leave, sooner you'll be coming back."

Tom took her into his arms and kissed her, then moved away, stepped a foot into a stirrup and swung up on the horse. "Gone only a week or two. If those men come back—"

"I'll be all right. Cora's man and some others will be keeping an eye on me."

He turned the mare to the street, then swiveled in the saddle to look back. "Maybe I shouldn't ought to go."

"For crying out loud, go! Better than moping around the place wondering about everything." She moved to the horse and gave it a slap on the flank.

With a farewell wave, Tom spurred the mare out to the street and turned it toward the town square.

Betty stood for a minute more, watching as horse and rider diminished into a distance and rode out of sight. With a sigh of the anxiety she had repressed, she moved up the steps to the back porch and entered the rear door of her home.

The city streets were dark. A flickering gaslight at the corner lengthened the shadow of Carl Parrish as he walked to the railroad company's building. He rapped on the main door and waited until the night guard came and unlocked it. "Here to see Sherwood. He's expecting me."

The guard nodded and stepped aside as the large man entered. Parrish moved to the stairway and started up, taking the steps two at a time, a big, agile man in a hurry. At the third floor, he strode down the corridor and paused at the lawyer's office door. He knocked twice, then turned the knob and walked in. "You wanted to see me?"

Langdon Sherwood was sitting at the conference table, a small lamp on a file cabinet the only illumination in the huge office. The attorney motioned to a chair at the table. Parrish crossed the room and sat across from the small man and waited for Sherwood to speak. The attorney stared out of the window for well over a minute before he turned to his visitor. "Well, if it isn't Mr. *Patrick Mahoney*. It seemed such a simple thing. Why in the world did you involve the woman?"

Parrish shrugged. "I thought it would bring him around if he turned us down."

"That was foolish," Sherwood said. "It could've been a straightforward deal, but the threat to his woman may have turned him into an adversary." He sat quietly for a few seconds more. "A most dangerous adversary I would say."

"My mistake," the big man admitted. "I should've just told him the situation and told him the name of that pigheaded fool."

"A fool, according to many witnesses, who Patterson actually threatened to kill," Sherwood interjected.

Parrish nodded, discomfited. "More than likely he'd have listened hard if I had told him straight out who it was. But things got out of hand before I had the chance." He shrugged. "My mistake, no doubt about it."

Sherwood nodded. "And mine for trusting the job to you."

"Let me handle it, Mr. Sherwood. I'll do it right this time."

"Perhaps it would be better if someone else talks to him."

Parrish shrugged.

"They were here, he and the woman. He was asking about that bogus Mahoney name you gave him and he was looking at that map. Seemed very curious about Placerville."

Parrish looked to the wall map. "Maybe he's heard I'd been hanging around over there."

The lawyer scowled in thought and nodded to the map. "Yes and, perhaps, there is something else he saw there."

"What could he possibly see?"

"I don't know," Sherwood responded. "For some reason, he wanted to know about the rail line ending there."

"Just talk, I reckon."

The lawyer shrugged.

"What do you want me to do?" Parrish asked.

"We may have to forget altogether about Patterson in this deal and do it another way . . . I'll have to think about that," Sherwood mused aloud. He stood quietly for several moments, then his lips pursed at a thought. "If he does start prowling around over your direction, he just might stumble right into where we want him."

Parrish smiled for the first time, correctly deducing the lawyer's notion. "Here's hoping he does. Maybe if and when he gets there and sees who and what's involved, we may not have to worry at all."

"If he comes nosing around, make sure he finds exactly who we want him to find."

Chapter Six

Tom spurred his mare and passed the slow moving wagon on the main street of Placerville, a place once called Hangtown in recognition of its previous penchant for neck-stretching activities.

Up ahead, the bell tower was a unique feature of the settlement. The tower contained a highly cherished alarm bell, shipped all the way from England, finally installed in a long overdue response to a series of fires way back in 1856 that had devastated the business district. Tom reined his horse to the side of the street, dismounted and tied up at the rail outside a narrow building with a window sign identifying it as the *Placerville Weekly Press*. He brushed his denim jacket and trousers and opened the door.

In the front office inside the building, a white-haired

elderly woman sat at a desk on Tom's left working at a ledger. Directly in front of him, a balding, middle-aged man with a pencil scribbled on a tablet. Beyond the front office, through an open door of a dividing partition, Tom could see another man in an apron working a large flatbed press; the rhythmic sound of the rotating cylinder and the pungent scent of printers' ink permeated the newspaper facility.

Both the man and the elderly woman looked up in expectation.

"Yes, sir," the balding man said. "Can I help you?"

"Maybe so, maybe not," Tom said hesitantly as he took off his hat. "I'm R.T. Patterson from Red Cliff. Got a freight-hauling business there. Probably ought to speak to the editor fellow."

"That'd be me, John Driscoll," the man said. Across the room, the elderly woman returned her attention to her work.

"Don't know rightly how to start," Tom said. "I got some questions and I ain't sure this is where I'll find the answers."

"Well, why don't you ask a few and see how it goes," Driscoll suggested and waved Tom to a chair beside his desk.

Tom sat down slowly, tentatively. "I'm looking for a man. Heard he's sometimes seen around these parts."

"What sort of man?"

"Big one, scar on his face that he tries to hide under his beard, dresses fancy, wears a suit and has one of them silk chokers around his neck. Thinks he's a swell."

The editor studied Tom for a short time. "Your tone, your manner . . . I take it you don't like this man?"

"I do need to talk with him."

"You mean him harm?"

Tom waved his hand away, palm up, a gesture of dismissal. "I'd rather it be handled by the law."

"What's this about?"

Tom shrugged. "I won't lie to you. He made a threat to my wife and was trying to get me into something bad. I've been a lawman myself. I mean to see that he answers for what he's already done to me and my family and for whatever he's planning to do."

"I don't know that I should get involved."

Tom nodded. "I'd understand but it's important. It might save somebody from getting killed."

"Killed?" The editor took a deep breath. "Now, for sure, I don't know that I should continue this conversation."

"Your call. If you can give me a lead, I'd appreciate it, but I won't push on it."

Driscoll took a long time considering his response. "I do know a fellow that might fit that description. Not a nice man."

"Does he go by the name of Mahoney?"

The editor shook his head. "Parrish, I think it is."

"Phony name, that figures. Is he here now? Live here?"

Again, Driscoll shook his head. "Haven't seen him

here in town for some time. I *have* heard he's been seen somewhere up around Virginia City." He paused. "I know nothing about him other than some things I've heard. Rumor has him in some nefarious dealings."

Tom lifted his eyebrows.

"Questionable dealings."

"Heard he might be doing some work for the railroad."

Driscoll slowly shook his head. "I don't know about that, but it wouldn't surprise me." He gave a wry smile. "People hereabouts are none too happy with railroads. Transcontinental went north some years back."

Tom nodded. "Worked for a spell on the UP and I recall how the word once was that it might come through Carson and down to here."

"It was a disappointment both to Placerville and to communities between here and Virginia City," Driscoll said. "There is a line from here down to Sacramento, but it isn't very busy these days. Southern Pacific or, now, Central Pacific has just about abandoned the line."

"Seems a shame."

"A loss of commerce to many towns. The railroads bring people and trade to towns. Those that got passed by just might dry up and blow away." The editor cocked his head in a questioning manner. "R.T. Patterson. Any chance that T stands for Thomas . . . as in Tom Patterson?"

"Possible."

"I've heard of you."

"Good side or bad?"

"As you said, you've been a lawman," the editor said. "Some writeups in my trade were about that business with the Jack Moss bunch back there in the Colorado gold camp. I guess it was on the good side."

"I'd hoped to leave that sort of business behind me," Tom told him. "The missus wants me to do the same here, but if this man you call Parrish was a threat to us once, he may be again."

The editor glanced up at the ticking clock on the wall.

"Best I be on my way," Tom said as he rose from the chair. "I do thank you for your time."

"Hope I've been of some help," Driscoll said as he rose. "If you're intent on finding that Parrish fellow, you might head on up to Virginia City."

"Just may do that."

They shook hands and Tom walked to the door, nodding to the elderly woman as he passed. Outside, he untied the reins of his horse and swung up on the saddle. He turned the mare back into the flow of traffic, wending his way through riders, wagons and buggies, heading east.

At the outskirts of the town, he reined Ginger to a halt and sat for a few minutes staring at the road leading into the mountains. "Maybe I'll take a look up there tomorrow," he said aloud. "Right after breakfast."

Parrish tugged the right rein to turn his horse-drawn buggy onto a weed-choked lane and waved the seven horsemen to follow. Less than a quarter of a mile later, he rounded a curve in the lane that led to the log ranch house ahead. The day before, he had found and rented it from the owner, an elderly widower now living in an old folks home in Placerville, a man too decrepit to live in country isolation any longer. Parrish had paid far too much for the ranch house. It was in a sorry state; windows broken, shingles missing, entry doors warped and difficult to close. Forty feet behind the house, a dilapidated barn had a definite lean to one side.

Still, it will have to do, Parrish judged.

He parked the rig next to the fractured and splintered corral rails and stepped out of the buggy to wave the seven men to dismount and encircle him.

"This is it?" one of the ruffians grumbled.

"Make do, boys," Parrish said brusquely. "It'll give us a roof over our heads . . . although I'm not saying the roof won't leak . . . but it'll give us a base close enough to do what we need to do. A few days and we'll be out of here."

"Thankee, Lord," a towheaded young man said in mockery. "Bless you for a holy, holy roof."

"Shut up, Johnny," Jim Ross spoke sharply. He was a wizened man of fifty who looked more like seventy. "Don't make fun of the Lord. What we do—"

"When was the last time you was praying to the Lord, old man?" the towhead cut in. "I don't 'spect He has much use for the likes of you and me, now does He?"

"You people are going to be bunking nose to nose for

a few nights, Johnny," Parrish admonished. "You start bickering now, you're of no use to me. Bring your traveling goods and let's go inside."

The men tied three horses to the hitching rail outside the ranch house and four others to the corral fence. Carrying bedrolls and following Parrish in single file, they traipsed into the house and looked around with dismay.

"All the windows is broke out, it ought to smell better," Tim, a lanky outlaw declared, pointing to the two narrow windows on the front wall.

The interior was mostly empty of furniture—only a table in the central room and a couple of rickety straight-backed wooden chairs. At one end of the house, a doorway led to an empty small bedroom with a high tiny window. The back of the room was a kitchen area, merely a waist-high slab of wood for a counter and some shelves hammered onto the wall above. A back door, the upper hinge broken, was half attached at the bottom, the top canting at an angle into the backyard. Between the back entrance and the barn, twenty feet away, a weathered-to-gray outhouse was at the end of a footpath.

"Bedroom will hold a couple, maybe three," Parrish said. "If it were me, I'd bed down right here in the main room. Those broken windows you're upset about will bring in some night breeze when you're trying to sleep."

"Ain't you staying here?"

"From time to time," Parrish responded. "I'll be moving back and forth . . . I got things to tend to in Placerville and thereabouts."

"Staying in a good feather bed in a fancy hotel, I betcha," came a caustic charge from a man, Paulie. "How long we gonna be?"

"Long as it takes," Parrish answered. "Things are going according to Hoyle, so it won't be but a few days at most."

"What's this all about?" Paulie asked. "That Patterson fellow really down here nosing around? Didn't we learn anything from the last time we butted heads with him?"

"Too many questions," Parrish replied. "Tell you what you need to know when the time comes."

"I don't like not knowing what I'm into," Paulie countered. "Like I didn't like Patterson bracing us back in that there hotel saloon when we thought *you* was holding all the cards."

"Paulie's making sense, boss," Ross put in. "He called our bluff once and—"

"Then pack up and leave," Parrish snapped. "Stay and you'll draw better wages than you can get anywhere else. Go and you won't get a penny."

The two men cast their eyes down and made no further comment, the others silenced and ill at ease.

"Make yourselves at home, boys," Parrish told them. "Be it ever so humble."

Chapter Seven

Deep in the earth, seismic convolutions and subsequent erosion had wrinkled the contours of the surface into level stretches, valleys, rocky outcroppings and rounded hills as a prelude to the towering Sierra Nevada Mountains. These lofty crags shaped a formidable barrier restricting travel and commerce, a major construction problem for the eventual construction of a transcontinental railroad. Passageways through or around the Sierras were relatively few and most not easy to traverse.

One of the access routes, a wagon road between Placerville and the Comstock Lode area had once been a busy thoroughfare, large wagons heading to California bringing cargos of silver and gold from Virginia City, Gold Hill, Silver City and American Flat. Also, stagecoaches and freight caravans, carrying food, building and mining supplies, streamed in both directions along with miners, tradesmen, peddlers, drifters, cardsharps and prostitutes.

When the transcontinental railroad was completed in 1869, a separate and independent rail line from Reno to Carson City was already in progress and finished in the same year. The traffic on the wagon road diminished as it shifted to the Virginia City and Truckee Railroad to interconnect with the transcontinental line, the riches of the Comstock Lode and most commerce now transported by trains west or to points east.

Tom had ridden out from Placerville shortly after sunup. It was a three-day ride to Carson City, even more if he took his time. He had wired Betty in the evening to tell her of his destination and promised to telegraph again upon his arrival. Although he encountered a few riders from time to time—a stagecoach and a couple of freight wagons heading west—the road was mostly deserted. He had never been in this part of California and never considered freight hauling in this area, the boom on this road long gone before his California arrival.

Just the other side of a small trading settlement, a rider spurred his dark bay horse to catch up to him. "Mind if I ride along with you?"

Tom's eyes searched the young man carefully. He appeared to be in his early twenties; a lean and sturdy medium build, clean-shaven with a tuft of blond hair showing beneath his wide-brimmed hat. The stock of a rifle in a saddle scabbard was visible on the right side of his mount and a holstered Colt rested on the young man's right hip.

"How far you going?" the young man asked.

"Nevada," Tom replied curtly, his gaze never wavering.

"If you'd rather, I'll drop back."

"That's all right. Glad to have the company."

The young man leaned from his saddle and extended his hand. "I'm Jed Porter. Heading up this way for a few miles."

"R.T. Patterson," Tom responded and shook Porter's hand.

"You on business, Mr. Patterson?"

Tom nodded.

"I live up in this area. Where are you from?"

"Back there aways."

The young man grinned, a merry look on his face. "I ask too damned many questions, don't I?"

"A few."

"I'll try to keep my mouth shut if you say so."

"I don't mind small talk."

"Beautiful country, don't you think?"

Tom nodded. "You get used to it."

"Me and my pa, we got a ranch up the road apiece in the valley. Really a nice spread. It's been in the family going on, now, five generations. It was one of the original Spanish grants made out to my great-great grandfather."

"Sounds like a durned good property."

"My pa's plumb crazy about the place. Wants to always keep it in the family and he won't hear otherwise. He was born there and says he wants to die there."

"You and your pa are lucky to have it."

"It's a mighty comfortable place, it really is." Young Porter leaned forward to make eye contact. "If you want, when we get there, we could put you up for the night. Better than sleeping out in the open or some fleabag place up the road."

"Kind of you," Tom acknowledged. "I'll give it some thought."

For the next few miles, they rode mostly in silence, only an occasional comment between them. The midday summer sun was high above as the horses labored up a steep grade, the heat bringing sweat in dark patches to the shirts of the two men. At the summit of the rise, the road fell away to a valley with a tree-shaded stream at its base. The horses began to trot at the sight and sense of water, Tom and Jed applying little restraint.

The two men dismounted and led the horses to the brook and let them drink. They moved upstream from the horses and removed their hats, scooping water from the cascading stream in cupped hands to splash it over their heads and bathe their faces.

"Damn, that feels good!" Jed exclaimed, soaking his neckerchief in the stream, then draping it over his head.

"Does indeed."

They sat with their backs against the trunks of adjacent poplars and watched as the horses stood in the stream dipping muzzles again and again into the water. After a few minutes, Tom rose and walked to the stream and led his horse back to the bank. "Ready to ride on?"

"Coming."

They mounted their horses and returned to the road. They walked their horses at a steady gait, letting their mounts regain strength and ease. The road curved through the valley between brown grass hillocks and, occasionally, small groves of trees.

For a couple of miles, Tom sat comfortably in his saddle, the swaying motion lulling him into a peaceful awareness of the scenic beauty of the land.

Jed's horse reared abruptly, the sound of the rifle shot instantly followed. Jed leaped clear as the animal shrieked in pain, thrashing and kicking as it staggered and plunged to the side of the road, whinnying in torment.

Tom spurred his mare into the trees as a second shot echoed. He swung down, pulled his rifle from the saddle scabbard, slapped the horse deep into the woods and dropped prone behind an earthen mound, his eyes seeking the shooter. "Leave the horse! Find cover!"

Jed scrambled to the other side of the road and hid behind a tree as his horse squirmed and kicked spasmodically and then lay still. "Where is he?" he yelled.

"Up that hill to the right, I think," Tom responded. "Won't be sure 'til he shoots again."

They waited.

Five minutes went by, then ten.

"Think he's gone?" Jed asked.

"Don't move. If we can wait, so can he."

"Maybe if we start shooting up there, we might flush him out."

"Waste of bullets. Ain't got any idea of where he might be."

"You said up on that hill."

"I might've been wrong."

"What'll we do?"

"Stay put. I ain't in no hurry to get myself killed."

"Who was shooting?"

"Danged poor is what they was," Tom said. "Two shots with a rifle and all they got was that poor damned horse."

Two hours later, Tom crawled to a large tree and stood up, sweeping his gaze into the woods behind him. "Keep your head down," he called softly. "I think he's gone, but I'm going to circle up around there and make sure."

Jed lifted a hand in a signal of compliance, then crouched closer to his tree.

Tom dashed from cover to cover, careful not to make a rhythm of his moves as he headed toward the hill. His greatest danger would be to cross the road so he moved through the trees on the left until he was well past the suspected position of the shooter.

I'm a damned fool, he decided as he emerged from the woods and ran full speed across the open road.

Made it!

Crouching low, his Colt in his right hand, he walked from tree to tree, his head moving from side to side, staring into the woods on either side, glancing behind as he advanced up the hill to the summit. He moved cautiously around the hilltop and came to a stop. He saw hoof prints on the earth, his eyes seeking the path of a horse's arrival and a trail of departure. He moved to a large fallen log and noticed the scrape across the bark where, possibly, a rifle barrel had been aimed. His notion was confirmed when he spied two cartridge shells on the ground nearby.

He started down the hill, still wary, his eyes searching. As he reached the road a few yards from the dead horse, he stepped behind a tree. "Jed, I'm coming out. Don't get nervous with your side arm."

"Is he gone?"

"Near as I can tell," Tom replied. "I'm coming out now." Slowly, he stepped out from behind the tree and walked forward. Jed rose from his hiding place and hurried to join Tom as they stood over the carcass.

"Damn!" Jed said and knelt to look at the chestnut gelding. "My pa will kill me for losing my horse."

"Better the horse than you."

Tom walked into the woods, found his horse and led her back to the road.

"What'll I do with him?" Jed nodded to the dead animal.

"Nothing you can do 'cept leave him," Tom said as he mounted his mare. "How far from your place?"

"Near three miles."

"Get your rifle and your saddle if you can," Tom instructed. "Stash your tack in the bushes over there where you can come back and get it." He motioned to the rump of his mare. "I can ride you double, but not with the saddle."

After unfastening the girth straps and much tugging, Jed pulled the saddle from the dead animal and dragged it to the undergrowth beside the road. Carrying the rifle in his left hand, he moved to Tom's horse and raised his right. Tom reached down to grasp Jed's hand and slipped his boot from the stirrup. Jed stepped into the stirrup as Tom heaved the young man up to swing over and straddle the horse behind him.

"All set?" Tom said over his shoulder.

"Let's go," Jed replied, looking back. "That was a damned good horse."

Tom jabbed the mare's flanks with his heels and the horse began its rhythmic gait.

"Were they shooting at you or me?" Jed asked.

"You got anybody mad at you?"

"Not that I know of."

"Probably, then, it was me."

"Any reason why?"

"Been shot at before," Tom responded. "I reckon you picked the wrong guy to go riding with."

"Be smart of you to stay off the road 'til morning."

Tom nodded. "I'd appreciate a place to stay the night."

In the late afternoon sun, the older man and younger one rode on the single horse, heading east, both wary of possible danger at each stand of trees and each bend of the road.

Chapter Eight

At Jed's direction, Tom turned his horse down a lane that branched from the main road. The late afternoon sun cast long shadows of the stubby trees and tall shrubs across the semi-arid ground. A considerable distance inland from the lush coast of California, the mountains and valleys they traveled gave a harsh preview of the desert lands ahead. Tom's eyes focused upon the deep shadows of a precipitous box canyon looming ahead. "We on your property yet?"

"Not yet."

Tom sensed the young man's hesitancy rather than hearing it. *Mighty poor grazing land*, he considered. *Maybe they run cattle at a different grassland location*.

A half-hour later, they came to a pair of posts on

either side of the lane, a hand-lettered sign on the right post declaring this portal the boundary of the Porter Ranch. Straight ahead, less than a quarter of a mile, he could see an adobe ranch house and several outbuildings framed against the box canyon and the vista of the Sierra Nevada range that lay beyond.

"It's no special spread like I let on," Jed admitted. "I was just putting on airs since we was just traveling a spell together."

"Makes no never mind to me," Tom responded.

"Sometimes I brag a bit, but I ain't no liar," the young man muttered.

"Do some bragging myself," Tom said.

"Used to be, it was a good-size ranch way back when." He shook his head. "Over the years, Pa's had to sell off some of it . . . a lot of it. Truth is, the place now is kinda run down, but he hangs on to the house and the canyon land behind it."

"If it makes a living, that's all you need."

"Well, we eat regular and got a couple of hands," Jed said. "None of us are ever going to get rich."

"Lived here all your life?"

The young man shook his head again. "Just a couple of years now. I lived with my ma in Missouri 'til she died. Ma and me moved there some time back after Pa came home from the army."

"Which army?"

"Union."

Tom turned in the saddle to face the young man. "I

was on the other side. If your old man would have a problem with that, best I just let you off and I'll ride on."

"Ain't no need to fret," Jed said hastily. "Offer still holds that we put you up for the night. Pa's away up there in the town of Kyburz and he might not even be back tonight."

"If he has hard feelings about rebs, best I not be there to provoke him."

"He ain't at all like that. His side won and, I reckon, he don't hold no grudges. He'd be mighty grateful for what you've done when we was getting shot at."

"Your property runs all the way back in the canyon?"

Jed nodded. "That's the best grazing land we got. When and if the rain does come, it greens up a mite."

Centered in the narrow mouth of the steep-walled box canyon, the ranch house was typical of the Mexican-style haciendas spread throughout California. Although modest in size, it was the most impressive structure on the property, a beige-toned adobe with a front portico including an overhang roof of brown tile. Fifty feet or more behind the house, a bunkhouse and a barn, both of dark, weathered wood, stood in contrast to the light-colored house. An empty corral occupied the space between the two outbuildings.

As they rode into the ranch enclosure, a stoop-shouldered, white-haired old man standing beside a wagon near the bunkhouse, turned. "Where's your horse, Jed?"

"Laying dead back on the road, Zeke," Jed said and

slipped off the horse. "Shot out from under me." He gestured to Tom. "This here is Mr. Patterson who helped me out and brought me home . . . and this is Zeke, one of our hands."

"Shot from under you?" the old man's leathery face puckered into a dour expression. "Lordy, who did a danged thing like that?"

"We don't know. Is Pa home yet?"

The old man shook his head. "Him and Sam ain't come home from Kyburz yet. Maybe not even tonight if Sam snuck off to having a drink—"

"Pa will skin him alive if he does." Jed turned to Tom. "Come down off your horse, Mr. Patterson. We got a spare room and it's far too late for you to get into Kyburz. Might as well stay, have a hot supper and get a good night's rest."

Tom glanced at the setting sun and nodded. "I thank you for the kind offer and I'll accept."

"Good!" Jed said. "Zeke'll take care of your horse."

"I'll do that myself," Tom said. "She's used to me and she'd be put out if somebody else was doing the care."

"Too late to do anything about my horse back there," Jed said to the wizened ranch hand. "You, me and Sam will handle that in the morning."

Tom dismounted and led Ginger into the barn. Horses occupied two of the six stalls; one looked old enough to probably belong to the elderly Zeke. Tom took his mare to an end stall and walked her inside. He took off the saddle, blanket and bridle, then inspected, picked and scraped each hoof. He found a stiff-bristled brush and began to carefully clean dried sweat and mud from the animal.

"There's rolled oats in the bin back at the door," the old man said as he entered the stall.

"I'll pay for what I use."

"No need," Zeke said, then stood silent for a few moments. "What was that about the horse being shot?"

Tom shrugged. "Beats me. Anything going on around here to be the cause of it?"

"No, not especially. Had some people looking around in the canyon some time back."

Tom gave him a sharp look. "On the ranch?"

"Yep, nosing around more than once at the back of the property. Mr. Porter didn't see 'em the first time, but he got pretty upset after that. Was going to go shoot 'em, that's how mad he was. They lit out and was gone before he could get on his horse and go after 'em."

"Any idea what they was looking for?"

"Nope. Boss knew, he never told me." He hesitated and then spoke with noticeable reluctance. "I wouldn't stay in the main house. The boy means well you staying the night, but his papa wouldn't like having a stranger in the house."

"I can move on."

"You could stay in the bunkhouse," Zeke told him. "There's room. Leave early in the morning. Maybe before he sees you."

"Not very hospitable, is he?"

The old man shook his head. "Hard man. Always angry." He paused. "I weren't here years ago but he come home from the war raging crazy. Run his wife and the youngster off with his temper."

"How long has Jed been back with him?"

"Not too long. Took him in, I 'spect, 'cause he had to, but he don't cut him no slack." He made a clucking sound. "When he finds out about the boy's horse, he'll be sore as hell."

Tom was silent for a long time. "I'll catch a little sleep in your bunkhouse. Wake me at first light if I don't get up myself."

"He won't make a fuss with you, I reckon," Zeke told him. "Likely take it out on the boy for bringing someone home."

"Even if that someone helped when people might have been shooting at that young man?"

The old man gave a humorless chuckle. "I can't explain him. All I can do is tell folks to stay clear of him."

"Why do you work for him?"

Again, the chuckle. "Feller, I'm an old man and I take work where I can find it. I'm too old to work at a good situation so I hang on here." He paused. "Someday, I'll do something he won't like and he'll kick me out." He turned away and then turned back. "I've cooked up a goulash if you and young Jed want to share." He gave a nod, ambled from the stall and out of the barn.

Tom finished brushing and feeding his horse and

walked out of the barn as Jed came through the back door of the house and hurried toward him. "Room's kinda cluttered. I'll—"

"No need to bother," Tom interrupted. "Your hand told me there's room in the bunkhouse. Also, he said he's got supper ready."

The young man looked relieved. "If it's okay with you?"

"Fine with me."

"Zeke's a good cook."

"Then, let's join him."

The sound of two shots snapped Tom out of his sleep. He reached for his Colt on a table beside his bunk bed, sat up and slipped his feet into his boots. He scanned the gloom of the bunkhouse; he was alone. His intent to sleep lightly had given way to a deeper slumber.

Tuckered out like an old man, he chided himself.

He stood, strapped his gun belt around his waist, grabbed his hat and moved cautiously toward the door of the bunkhouse. After supper with young Jed and Zeke, he had bid them good-night and retired to an empty bed in the open-room sleeping quarters. He had dozed at first, stirred when Zeke bedded down, and awakened again near midnight at the sound of the arrival of Jed's father and the other ranchman.

The windows admitted a faint light of the moon; Tom estimated the time shy of four o'clock. He opened the door a crack and looked outside. Five feet away, Zeke's nightshirted body lay sprawled on the ground. Near the back of the ranch house, another body lay still in a small black puddle of what Tom assumed to be blood.

Tom came out of the bunkhouse in a crouch and moved to the old man. He knelt beside him, his left hand seeking Zeke's neck. There, he felt the regular beat of the heart and heard the even breathing. In the moonlight, he could see a bloody gash on the scalp through the sparse white strands.

Out cold. Hell of a thing to do to an old man.

A commotion at the ranch house drew Tom's instant attention. A tall, heavy man, a dark figure against the light adobe walls, came out of the house and moved to kneel over the still body close by. A moan began and escalated into a wail of sorrow. "Tom Patterson! You've killed my boy! Come out, you dirty backshooting trash!"

Young Jed? Killed? God in heaven!

"Where are you, Tom Patterson? Show yourself, you damned coward!" The man took three steps forward, turning his face left and right, scanning the yard and outbuildings, then started moving forward, wary, a revolver held high at his chest.

Now able to see his face and hearing the strident voice . . . something about the man seemed familiar, memories racing through Tom's mind: *Without the beard, thirty pounds lighter, shoulders square, not rounded, back ramrod straight . . . and a blue uniform with a captain's bars on the tunic collar! Mass murderer!*

"Portee, not Porter," Tom whispered. "Captain Edward

Portee." Rage surged and Tom raised his revolver, aimed and then lowered it again.

Jed's father peered into the darkness of the bunkhouse shadow, leveled the revolver and fired, the shot blasting into the siding of the bunkhouse a yard to his left. Another bullet slapped into the doorframe beside him. Tom stepped back inside, took careful aim and fired at the advancing man's feet.

Jed's father stopped.

"Keep coming and you're dead!" Tom called loudly. "I didn't kill your son—"

Four more shots thundered through the door, followed by many clicks of the hammer on empty chambers.

Tom stepped out once more. "I didn't kill your son."

"You're lying . . . you did it to get even!"

In the moonlight, he could see the man feeding bullets into his revolver.

Shoot him! Shoot him while you got the chance!

Tom stepped forward and raised his revolver, cocked the hammer, then lowered it again.

"Portee!" he called. "I ain't gonna kill ya though Lord knows I got the right! But if you don't put your gun down right now, I'll put one in one leg, maybe in the other one too!"

The dark silhouette continued to load, ignoring him.

"Well, damn!" Tom said softly. He raised his revolver and aimed at the man's left leg.

Two shots came from a different sector of the ranch. Tom ducked instinctively and then realized neither was aimed at him. Instead, Edward Portee staggered back, dropped to his knees and toppled facedown in the yard, his revolver flying from his hand.

Before Tom could react, a bullet buzzed past his face. He dropped to the ground and rolled to his left, seeking cover behind the wagon. Bullets followed him, stitching a path, two coming within inches. Lying prone behind a wheel, Tom's eyes searched the central part of the ranch complex and saw the flash of a gun by the barn and that of another at the side of the ranch house. He realized the wagon gave scant cover and a hit was likely at any instant. He rolled up into a crouch and fired his revolver three times in rapid succession at the corner of the ranch house and dashed for the corral. He dove to the ground again and slid under the lower rail, then rose and ran to the side of the barn. Momentarily safe from gunfire from the house, he hurried along the barn to the back of the corral. In the open space between the ranch and the corral, there was movement, two shadowy figures scurrying into position to target him again. Tom went under the back fence and took refuge behind the rear corner of the barn. At the opposite corner, a man appeared, revolver raised to fire. Tom snapped a shot that skipped across the plank wood siding above the head of the man who ducked immediately out of sight. Tom hesitated for only a moment, then ran as fast as he was able into the shrub brush terrain, bending low, zigzagging through a few meandering cattle as bullets whizzed dangerously near.

Two hundred yards from the ranch, Tom stopped

running and, still crouched low, raised his head and looked back. Out of pistol range, he knew that a rifle shot could still reach him. He could see five men at the ranch, now in the open, obviously as aware as he that a shot from a handgun was useless. They would be coming soon, most likely armed with rifles, fanning out across this vale to hunt him down.

Getting back to his horse was out of the question. Tom looked left and right, looking for an escape route. To his left, tumbled boulders from the steep canyon side were a few hundred yards away—to his right, a far greater distance. Tom made his decision immediately and, still bending low, began to run toward the nearest option.

There was an outcry as he was seen and, as expected, a bullet from a rifle cut the air behind him. Galvanized, Tom came erect to run at greater speed, disregarding the sounds of repeated gunfire and the whispers and smacks of bullets coming close.

He reached the first boulder and ducked behind it, peering around it to see if he was being pursued. The sun, still below the horizon, was beginning to brighten the landscape and he could see the men clearly now although at a considerable distance. They had stopped their progress and were staying far away from Tom's shooting range. Tom took bullets from his belt and reloaded his Colt as he watched the men. One man, larger than the others, was in conversation with another.

Parrish, Tom guessed and knew he was right. Even

at this distance, the size and characteristics of his movements confirmed his supposition.

The man with Parrish turned and started trotting toward the ranch house.

How many men between me and getting out of here? And going for more? What have I got myself into?

He looked up at the great height of the canyon walls. Four, five, six hundred feet, maybe more, he estimated. He studied the nearest rock face, seeking some sort of an accessible path to the top. There were several vertical gullies indented deeply enough in the canyon precipice to give him some cover from gunfire if he would dare to climb.

Dare to climb? Tom shook his head. *Lord knows if this tired old body can do it.*

Chapter Nine

Bending low, Tom worked his way through the rock piles and large boulders to the base of the canyon wall. Wary of his pursuers, he split his attention between glancing back at them and seeking the easiest climb to the top. Water of the ages had poured down the precipice sides, cutting channels, five reachable on this wing of the canyon without exposing him to the men behind him. He studied each of the deep-set furrows and selected two as the best choices. Both gullies appeared to be reachable from the canyon floor to the high rim. Close together, both were vertical troughs with a good number of coniferous trees and plant outgrowths rooted in the cracks and fractures that could aid in the climb and, possibly, even hide him from the sight of the men below.

Tom moved to the base of the left gully and pushed his way through the gnarly evergreens into the faint light of the dark cleft. Eons of rainfall had washed small stones and pebbles down the chute to form a jumbled mound at the bottom of a nearly straight-up channel to the top. He holstered his Colt and bent down to use hands and feet to scramble up the pile to the rock face of the gully. For a few seconds, he was stymied: The granite channel was wide and smooth at the bottom with neither a place for a foot to step nor a handhold to grasp. Three feet above his head, the chute narrowed and the sides were jagged and irregular. Tom crouched low and leaped for a stumpy shrub rooted in a fissure, caught it with one hand, then with the other, hoping it would support his weight. He pulled himself up as it threatened to break and reached for an inch-wide ridge. With his left fingers on the little edge, he reached higher with his right for a chink in the rock surface. With arm strength alone, he pulled himself higher, one handhold after another until his left boot found a rock protrusion and he settled on it carefully, easing the strain on his arms and shoulders.

"Good Lord Almighty," he muttered, almost a prayer. "I ain't hardly started and I'm plumb wore out already."

He looked at the steep climb ahead, sighed and began to labor up the channel. *Boots for climbing, for crying out loud!*

He touched the toe of his left boot to a higher slim rock shelf. Tentatively, he put part of his weight on that foot while hanging tight to right and left handholds. He moved up and found a stretch of the chute above to have jagged rock protrusions he could scale with greater ease and pace.

After several minutes, he stopped to rest with one foot on a substantial ledge and looked down, estimating he had reached a height of sixty feet or more from the base. The sun had not yet risen above the horizon and very little light penetrated the fissure in the canyon wall. With the shielding outgrowth of crevice shrubbery, he doubted the men below could see him. Keeping out of sight within the darkness of the gully, he could see them, still keeping their distance from the boulders.

They'll figure me out soon and they'll come. Gotta get higher before they spot me, gotta get way up before the sun shows me.

He looked up for places to put his hands and feet and started climbing the gully again. The ascent was painfully slow, the vegetation thinning as he moved up the trough. His muscles ached and trembled, his fingers becoming raw. The deep gloom that hid him from view was brightening; direct sunlight on the canyon wall would soon reveal him. He glanced down and was surprised at the great height he had managed. The men below were miniaturized and were moving close to the base of the canyon wall. They were looking up to scan the fissures—now knowing he was in one of them. *If a rifle shot don't get me clean, a fall will do me for sure.*

He continued climbing, his eyes searching the surface of the rocks on either side of the steep, near-vertical trough for places to step, places to grasp, his gaze concentrated on his immediate surrounding area.

Five feet, then ten, fifteen, twenty—

Tom raised his head in disbelief. The fissure ended in a flattened catch basin below a huge granite overhang that jutted out from the canyon wall. He pulled himself up onto the uneven surface, avoiding the shallow pool of stagnant water in the middle of the cratered recess. Countless millennia of rain had cascaded from the lip of the overhang to create this small cavity, the backsplash wearing away the rock face behind the pool. There was not enough room to stand, but it was a relief to sit and rest from the strain of climbing.

Tom was not relieved as he surveyed his predicament. The overhang could be climbed only if he were a fly and able to defy gravity. *I can't go up and I can't go down and I can't stay here.*

He leaned out and looked to his right, looking for the gully that paralleled this one on the canyon wall. From his point of view, there appeared to be a gap some twenty feet away. Looking down, he could track the fissure angling up from the base. *If it goes to the top, how do I get there?*

Several feet below him, there was a three-inch wide rock shelf that extended for nearly ten feet before it curved out of sight. Above it, there were cracks and protrusions that could provide handholds.

The bad part was that the sun was breaking over the horizon and intense light was touching the rim of the canyon only thirty feet above his crossing path.

Tom rubbed his arms to massage away the aches, then carefully descended and moved out of the gully, stretching his right hand to a chink on the sheer canyon wall. He stepped his right foot onto the ledge and then his left. He looked down and immediately regretted his folly, sheer terror overwhelming him. "Never knew I was 'fraid of heights . . . now I do," he muttered, and fixed his eyes strictly on the stone surfaces to his right.

He inched his way across the ledge, hugging the wall, hands touching and exploring, finding finger holes, cracks and chinks to cling to. He sidestepped along the ledge and nearly panicked when it disappeared as he moved around an angle. He froze and carefully scanned the precipice. Two feet above and a foot to his right, a six-inch-wide ledge extended for a short distance across the rock face. A tight fracture line was the only rift below the ledge in the smooth stone surface and so tightly compacted, there was no room at all for a hand or even fingers. Tom pressed his face against the wall and closed his eyes, visualizing and dreading what he had to do.

Slowly, carefully, he bent his knees and lowered his body into a crouch, feeling the gravity pulling as the center of his weight shifted out over the edge of the precipice. He held his hands against the granite, fingertips digging into tiny grooves to hold him to the wall.

Tom gathered his body and his will, leaped high and reached for the ledge with both hands. His clawed fingers hooked the top of the ledge, the right hand hanging on, the left slipping, then hooking again. Tom dangled, feeling the strain of his weight trying to pry his fingers from the stone. He rested for a fraction of time and then chinned himself up to the ledge, his eyes searching for another handhold. He whipped his left hand to a crack an arm length higher and caught a fingerhold to lever himself up to a knee on the ledge. A couple of other handholds enabled him to rise and plant both feet on the rock shelf.

"There he is!" a cry came from far below.

Tom moved immediately, edging his way across the face of the wall, his movements decided in haste, his progress abysmally slow. The scatter of exploding rock erupted a half-foot from his left shoulder followed by the report of a rifle. Another bullet blasted the granite a few inches from his head, a gritty spray peppering his face. Tom wiped his sleeve across his eyes and continued his slow traverse to his right, cringing in anticipation for the next and fatal shot. *Six feet ahead, the gully is there, all the way up!*

Reaching it was a different matter. The ledge beneath his feet ended abruptly and the face of the precipice ahead was a smooth plane with no cracks or protrusions for his hands. The only protuberance was a rounded knob of granite two feet below and a little more than halfway across the distance.

Two more bullets shattered the rock surface on either side of him. Tom tucked his right foot behind his left and pushed off on it, leaping over the abyss for the knob, his left boot sole hitting the top of the rounded stone and springing him forward, catapulting him into the neighboring furrow. He started to slide immediately, his hands grasping, reaching for anything to stop the fall.

Tom's left hand caught a small branch of a fir tree outgrowth and swung him to a stop, his right hand flailing and seeking another support. He found it in the same crack at the base of the tree and hung on. He looked down and found a rocky outcropping on which he could rest his left foot. He hugged the wall to rest his body, feeling the pounding of his heart and the sharp pains of scrapes and bruises that seemed everywhere, especially in his hands and elbows. Rifle bullets were still hitting and ricocheting into the area around him, but not as close as before.

Wearily, Tom lifted his head and looked up the gully. *Thirty feet to the top!*

Slowly, determinedly, Tom resumed his climbing. It took ten minutes for him to reach the top of the trough. There had been only a few additional shots from below and he guessed that the curvature of the canyon wall meant that they could not see him unless they moved back from the precipice and out of practical marksmanship range.

He pulled himself to the summit of the ridge and

looked over the edge. Below, the men were moving away, heading back to the ranch house. He stood erect and turned to survey the height and depths of the mountain terrain he would have to descend. He walked along the ridge for several steps to look for the easiest way down.

The rattle of a snake brought him to an immediate standstill.

The snake, basking in the early morning sun, struck short and missed.

The toe of Tom's boot caught the recoiling diamond-back and sent it flying over the edge of the canyon. "Not after what I've been through, you sleepy sidewinder!"

Carl Parrish entered the back door of the ranch house and walked into the kitchen where Jed, bare to the waist, was at a washbasin sponging away the animal blood from his head and shoulders.

"You get him?" Jed asked.

"Might've winged him," Parrish answered. "He was climbing up one of those canyon gullies."

Jed turned. "Might have? You don't know?"

Parrish shook his head.

"Sherwood was right. You *are* worthless."

"I don't take that from you or Sherwood," Parrish said sharply. "Who the hell would think he'd climb a damned cliff in the dark and make it?"

"You should've shot him right here when you had the chance. You should've shot him first, then Pa."

"Bullcrap," Parrish countered. "The plan was for the two of them to have a shoot-out. It was supposed to look like it was between the two of them 'cause they hated each other. For a few minutes there, it looked like it was going to be the real thing." He shook his head. "He never came far enough out of the shadows of the bunkhouse where we could get a good shot at him."

Jed reached for a towel and dried himself. "You still let him get away."

"The man's got nine lives."

"Your excuse for doing a bad job. By the way, you owe me a horse. All you were supposed to do is fire a couple of close shots down there to spook him into staying off the road at my place."

"Your nag moved into my line of fire," Parrish responded defensively. "I was aiming at the ground. You shouldn't have been there."

"You came too damned close to me and I ain't forgetting that at all. On your way out, get a rope around that nag's neck and drag it way into the brush where no one can see." Jed walked to the door and looked out. "How soon will the law get here?"

"It'll take some time. Somewhere before noon, I reckon."

"Zeke?"

"Didn't have to shoot him, but it worked out just fine. He got up early and was heading for the privy before anything started. One of my boys knocked him in the head with his gun barrel so as not to make a shooting noise. The way it is now, it makes it look like Patterson took him from behind."

Jed frowned. "How bad is he?"

"He's still laying out there, but I 'spect he'll be all right."

"Maybe we ought to go ahead and shoot him to be on the safe side."

Parrish frowned and shook his head. "Be hard to explain that bash on the head and being shot to boot. 'Sides, from what we know about Patterson, shooting your old man makes sense and killing the hired hand ain't necessary."

Jed nodded. "All right, you and the rest clear out before Sam gets back with the sheriff. We'll say that Patterson shot Pa and then Sam and me chased him off. We'll get a warrant for him, dead or alive, and a posse to make sure it's the first not the last."

Parrish smiled. "Don't underestimate this man, Jed."

Jed responded with a mocking smile of his own. "You make mistakes, Carl. I don't."

After Parrish and his men rode away, Jed came out of the house. He walked to his father's body and stood over it. "Wouldn't listen, would you?" he spat the words. "We could've been living rich and pleasured in 'Frisco or anywhere we wanted, but, no, this is where you wanted to live and die." He kicked the rib cage of the dead man. "Well, you got your wish, didn't you?"

He regarded the corpse for a few seconds more, then

moved toward the bunkhouse. He paused and knelt down beside the old man who was beginning to stir. Jed watched Zeke's hands twitch and heard the low moans of hurt.

"Coming around, Zeke?"

Zeke's eyelids fluttered and the moans began to change to whispers.

Jed looked at the gash on the ranch hand's head and reached for his revolver. "Might as well finish up what's been started."

Chapter Ten

He remembered the small stream running red with the blood of bluebelly and reb soldiers lying dead and dying in the water and on the banks. It was a lesser tributary of the Rapidan River in the tangled undergrowth and forest of what was called the Wilderness in Virginia. It was early May in 1864 and Grant's main army had begun the assault. For three days, there had been tremendous slaughter on both sides, the warfare nearly decimating Tom's Texas cavalry unit.

"We gotta give it up, boys," Sergeant Casey Beckman said. He was lying on the ground on his left side, a hand with a crimson rag pressed to a seeping wound in his right thigh. "We got no choice."

With officers killed, every horse worn or blown to death, supplies and ammunition gone, Tom and twelve others were isolated on a hummock amidst a dense stand of trees, constantly aware of Yankee troop movements all around them. Occasionally, they'd see the blue-uniformed soldiers moving in groups or individually through the forest, easy targets had there been bullets for their guns.

"Anybody got anything white?" Sergeant Beckman asked.

One of the men pulled a soiled handkerchief from his hip pocket.

"Tie it on your rifle," the noncom instructed and waited while the private attached the stained cloth to the barrel of his weapon. With considerable pain, he rose to his feet and motioned for the others to stand. "Toss them guns, boys, side arms too." He nodded approval as the soldiers dropped their weapons and then motioned the young man with the white-flagged rifle to a forward position. "Hold that rifle high and lead on," Beckman said. "We'll follow."

The young man swept the woods with a fearful gaze and stepped out in a slow and hesitant walk. One of the soldiers slipped his shoulder under Beckman's arm and, together, they began a lurching march behind the leader. The rest of the men fell in and walked forward, hands held high above their heads, Tom reluctantly last to join the march.

They moved through the woods without seeing an enemy soldier, each man puzzled and worried because, for three days, the woodland had been alive with firefights, artillery bursts, rebel cries, shouts of defiance and screams of severe pain.

Tom walked with his hands held high, uncomfortable with his vulnerability, worried that a fusillade of gunfire was likely to erupt from unseen trigger-happy Union shooters. If they were lucky enough to be taken prisoner without incident, he would be relieved. The war was going badly even though Lee and his generals were still making a desperate fight of it.

When he had joined the Confederate Army, a yearning for adventure had been the folly of his exuberant youth. He had had only a vague notion of the southland's cause and, as the war exacted such an awful count in horrid deaths and hideous wounds it didn't seem noble at all. He had killed his share of bluebellies and, at his hands, watched death glaze the eyes of frightened baby-faced youngsters.

"Column halt!" Sergeant Beckman commanded as they entered a clearing.

They stopped walking and stood still.

From the surrounding trees, Union infantrymen materialized, more than forty, and surrounded the small group.

Tom realized the surrender was a mistake. This enemy company was made up of rough, loutish conscripts likely recruited from the slums of Northern cities.

"Get in a goddamn line, you sorry-assed, Southern bastards!" shouted a burly, unshaven soldier with corporal stripes on his filthy uniform. He ripped the white-flagged rifle from the frightened youth and jabbed it, butt first, into the young soldier's stomach. As the youngster doubled in pain and gasped for breath, another Yankee soldier kicked him on his buttocks and brought hearty laughter and raucous glee from the ragtag Union soldiers. Tom and his comrades were shoved and punched into a line by their profane and taunting captors.

The physical and verbal abuse came to an abrupt end as two Union officers came into the clearing. In the lead was a captain, a swift-striding tall man with a strong aura of command. Behind him, a young lieutenant directed his attention to the disorderly infantrymen standing at near attention. The tall captain gave his men only a cold glance and then his eyes fastened and remained on the line of disheveled and disheartened Confederates.

"Who's in charge?" the captain asked.

"Me, sir," Sergeant Beckman spoke clearly. "Under the articles of war—"

"Shut up!" the captain cut in and turned to his subordinate officer. "Lieutenant Noland! How far to command?"

The young officer shook his head. "No way of knowing, sir. A far distance, maybe."

The captain nodded and stood silent for more than a minute. "We can't be slowed by prisoners."

The lieutenant showed his puzzlement. "Captain Portee? I'm not sure—"

"Shoot them."

No one moved.

No one spoke.

The junior officer cleared his throat. "Sir, I don't go along with this—"

"Shoot them, Noland!" Captain Portee repeated the command. "Select a firing squad—"

"Captain!" Sergeant Beckman interrupted. "You can't do this!"

The tall officer drew his revolver from his holster, cocked it and fired point-blank into the Confederate noncom's face. He cocked it again and stepped to the next man and repeated an act of execution.

Panic erupted as Tom and his terrified comrades bolted and ran into the woods. The Union soldiers reacted quickly, raising rifles to fire at the fleeing rebels. Three fell on Tom's right, another man on his left. Tom glanced over his shoulder and saw the captain's revolver aimed at him and the lieutenant's hand whip out to knock it aside.

Tom heard bullets buzzing past, thumping into the trees as he ran. He continued to run at full speed, low branches of trees and thorny shrubs whipping his face and body. He could see no others of his company and knew not whether anyone else had escaped the deadly fire.

Exhausted, with the executioners far behind, Tom came to a stop and leaned against a tree. He gulped for air, long wheezing draughts pulled into his labored lungs. He rested for another five minutes and waited for strength to return.

"Soldier?"

Tom turned and was relieved to see a gray uniform, not a blue one.

"Soldier?" the Confederate junior officer repeated. "Where's your unit?"

Tom shook his head. "Shot to hell, sir," he said in a hoarse whisper. "Maybe all gone."

The officer regarded him for a few moments, then gave a sidewise motion of his head. "Join up with our company back there."

Ten months after Lee's surrender, a court-martial convened at Norfolk, Virginia. A charge of multiple murders of Confederate prisoners by Captain Edward Portee was brought by a Captain Joseph Noland who had been a lieutenant, second in command, of Portee's company during the Battle of the Wilderness. The charge, skillfully defended as prejudiced and untrue, was dramatically strengthened by the appearance of Thomas Patterson, the sole Confederate survivor of the massacre. Despite the scowls and disdain of the presiding Union officers, Tom's separate testimony agreed substantially with Captain Noland's. At the end of his devastating statement, Tom remembered Portee's glare of absolute hatred. After several days of deliberation, Captain Edward Portee was found guilty, demoted and dishonorably discharged.

"If you don't kill him, I will," Tom said softly, repeating the threat he had made aloud at that court-martial years ago. It was a threat decried and resented by the conquerors and widely reported in the newspapers covering the sensational trial. Of course, the army hadn't delivered a death sentence and, as years passed, neither had he.

Now, Tom stood at the summit of the granite uplift that formed the back wall of the canyon. He looked down: At the base of the steep slant, a scenic valley stretched far into the distance.

And, finally, he began to understand.

Many years ago when Central Pacific's chief engineer, Theodore Judah, had explored and surveyed five or more possible routes for the transcontinental railroad, Tom wondered if he had ever seen this possibility. The inverted stone wedge below him was not an impassable obstruction; a tunnel through the relatively narrow base was doable. Thousands of Chinese laborers that had picked and blasted the way through the high Sierras were still available in San Francisco and other California coastal cities. After a couple or even three years to tunnel through this negligible barrier, it would open the way to this valley and provide a rail connection to the southern end of Lake Tahoe where, even now, fancy hotels and resort communities were envisioned. Depending upon where the valley turned, a rail line here could possibly revitalize the dreams of the merchants in many bypassed communities between Placerville and Carson City.

What would it be worth? Millions? And the killings

at the ranch? He thought he knew the answer but there were more immediate concerns. He walked along the narrow plateau atop the canyon, his eyes seeking a gradual path to lower ground. Once down, wherever he would go in hostile territory, people would be searching for a man alone, on foot. *Bett was right. Why didn't I just let it go?*

Chapter Eleven

"This Patterson," Sheriff Willis Morgan began, "joined up with you on your way home?"

"Seemed like a nice sort of a fellow," Jed responded. "I had no idea. Asked if he could spend the night." He paused. "I saw no reason why not." He paused again, a wince of regret on his face. "I had no idea."

The sheriff, an outsized and weathered man in his early fifties, had arrived just a few minutes before, the mid-morning sun high in the sky. The bodies still lay in the yard between the ranch house and the bunkhouse, the blood of each congealed and turning black. Three deputies were standing in idle poses, waiting for their boss to give instructions.

"Gus," Sheriff Morgan called to one of them. "No need to let them stay in the sun. Get a buckboard out of the barn and we'll tote them back to the undertaker in town." He turned an apologetic face to Jed. "It might be better if you go inside while we take care of things."

"It's all right, Sheriff," Jed replied. "What's done is done. What I want to know is what is going to happen about the man that killed my pa and poor old Zeke."

"You know why he did this?"

"I heard my pa call him by his name. How he knew his name, I had no idea. I hadn't mentioned it."

"Tell me what happened."

"Pa came home late last night. He went in the house and I told him we had a fellow staying for the night in the bunkhouse. Pa went out to see about him and Patterson was waiting for him. Pa tried to draw but he already had his gun out and never gave him a chance."

The lawman clucked his sympathy and looked to the summit of the canyon. "Hell of a climb," he mused aloud. "You and Sam the only ones between him and the road out?"

Jed nodded. "We damned sure weren't going to let him past us."

"Seems like it'd been a lot easier to circle past the two of you than shinnying up that mountain." He sighed. "Well, since he's on foot, he'll have a hell of walk to get out of the country. When we get back to town, I'll get a posse together and I'll wire the law in neighbor towns."

"Where do you think he'll come down?"

"Hard to say. He'll likely want to get back to the road somewhere and we'll post men east and west. That's about all we can do."

"I want to be on that posse."

The sheriff pursed his lips. "I'll have to do some thinking about that."

"Aren't you going in after him?"

Morgan put his hand to his chin. "Hard country. Even if we was to come near finding him, he'd have the advantage. He could see us and hide long before we see him." He shook his head. "Best we wait for him to come out. Even if he gets by us now, he'll show up somewheres and that's where we'll get him."

"I don't like that, Sheriff. I don't like that at all."

"You're rightly upset, boy," Morgan counseled. "I understand you want to get even, but you best let us do what we know how."

"I want him dead, Sheriff."

Morgan didn't answer immediately, his gaze fastened upon the top of the canyon. "He'll likely die up there in that back country. If and when he does come out, we'll probably have a fair trial and a necktie party."

"Have my way, Sheriff, we don't need a trial."

The lawman gave young Porter a stern look. "I'll say it again . . . let us do what we know how. You've got some chores to do to bury your dad and the other fellow."

Jed didn't respond for a long while, then a sheepish, shy smile came back to his boyish face. "Of course,

Sheriff, whatever you say. I'll count on you to do what's right."

Tom stepped around the sun-bleached bones of a cow's skeleton in the rocky gulch. *Poor damned thing trying to find a way out. Just like me.*

The descent from the mountain heights had not been easy, involving some slipping and sliding. The landscape on the other side of the box canyon did include the valley bordered by a range of high rounded hills and jagged crags. He considered an escape path through that valley, but that would likely take days or weeks to explore and time was too important. *Find Parrish*, he decided. *No matter the risk, gotta find him.*

To his right and left, numerous trails led into rugged terrain. Although reluctant to travel rough country, he entered and trudged through a narrow arroyo and wondered if it would come to a dead end or, he hoped, open to a path of escape. His feet were sore from the uncommon tortures of climbing up and down vertical surfaces. He continued walking along the dry streambed for several minutes and came to a channel fork where another gully from the right joined the gulch. He paused to consider: The new branch seemed to rise into the mountains on a steeper plane than the other. He made his decision and followed the ravine to his left.

Five minutes later, he walked into a small open area with a pool of fresh water beneath a trickling waterfall fed from the rocky bluffs above. When a significant rain or spring snowmelt came, the pool would fill and overflow and the arroyo he had traveled would likely become a path for a fierce torrent surging down to the valley.

Tom looked for a way out of the basin and was gratified to see a modest hill that seemed an easy climb to whatever lay beyond. He walked to the edge of the pool and cupped his hands to catch water from the falling stream and drank again and again. He sat under the shade of a rocky overhang, his first rest in hours. *Could I live in here for a spell? Won't die of thirst. Shells left for shooting whatever game prowls this backcountry if I had a way of cooking it. Eat it raw if I had to.* He shook his head. "Ain't fair to Betty," he said aloud. "She'd be fretting and thinking I was dead."

Reluctant to leave the cool shade and cold water, Tom rose and walked toward the hill. At its base, he found signs of a trail where animals or, perhaps, humans had climbed before. The path wound up toward the summit with numerous fir trees along either side to give his arms the leverage he would need to propel himself up the slope.

At the top of the hill, looking down, he could see the openings of three more gulches ahead, each one winding and disappearing into the mountains.

Which one?

He followed the path down the hill and studied the ground. The faint trail disappeared, but Tom continued to move forward, bent low, his eyes searching.

He stopped and stood erect.

Trail in all three, take your pick.

He reached to the ground and selected three distinctive small stones. He turned his back and, all at the same time, tossed them over his shoulder. He turned again and walked forward, eyes sweeping the terrain. Straight ahead, two stones lay squarely in line with the entrance to the central arroyo.

Two out of three. Good choice as any.

As the long evening shadows disappeared and the dim light of dusk grew darker, Tom examined the walls of the arroyo, looking for snake holes or other openings for unwelcome mountain denizens. He selected a small depression still warm from the rays of the afternoon and evening sun and settled into it. The night would be cold and he was glad of the light denim jacket even though it would provide scant comfort. With his hat tilted forward, his head touching the stone behind him, he hugged his arms across his chest and watched the twilight become night. He listened to the sound of wind and the cries of night birds winging through the starlit skies. Somewhere, in the distance, a coyote gave a short bark and then a long and mournful howl.

Tom closed his eyes and waited for sleep.

Chapter Twelve

Early in the day, Jed Porter rode Tom's horse along the wagon road, spurring the mare to a gallop as he approached a small group of mounted men. "Morgan!" he shouted. "Anything?"

Sheriff Morgan broke off his conversation with a posse member, plainly irritated at the interruption.

"Well?" Jed asked as he reined up beside the lawman.

"Nothing yet," Morgan responded, not bothering to keep the annoyance out of his voice. "Told you I'd let you know."

"Can't blame me for asking," Jed shot back, his own temper evident. "We ought to go in."

Morgan sighed. "My God, boy. You ain't got no idea of how much tough riding is back in those mountains.

We could hunt for days and not find him, likely cripple a horse or even a man or two."

"'Spect to find him with all of you sitting in a bunch in the middle of the road?"

Morgan sighed again. "Look here, young man. Each of these men have been spread out up and down the road all day yesterday and all night. Same up the road."

"And now they're all here."

Morgan nodded. "That's a fact . . . and Patterson might be sneaking past 'em right now a mile down this way or a couple of miles that way."

"And that don't worry you?"

"What the hell can we do about it, boy? I ain't got an army to post men every ten feet for miles and miles. All we can do is patrol along the way just in case someone sees him. If that happens, he fires a shot and we all come running." He snorted his exasperation and swiveled in his saddle to address one of his men.

"You're a poor excuse for a sheriff!"

Morgan turned back with a quick intensity that made Jed recoil in alarm. He spurred his horse close to Jed's and, for a long moment, the older man seemed ready to strike. "Listen to me," Sheriff Morgan said evenly. "Only because you just lost your father I won't slap you out of that saddle. Talk to me once more like that and I'll loosen your teeth. Now, you git yourself home or to the funeral parlor or to wherever you got things to tend to. Now git!"

Disdainfully, the lawman turned his back to Jed as all

men of the posse smirked and chuckled. Sweeping them with an angry glare, Porter turned his horse and slapped the reins on the mare's rump to galvanize her into a gallop.

"Kid's got a mouth on him," one deputized cowboy ventured.

"His old man was a bad-tempered fool," Sheriff Morgan said. "I guess the apple don't fall far from the tree."

Tom continued his trek through the maze of ravines, rifts and narrow mountain passages. From the sun's position in the sky, he was working his way to the south, but he had no idea of where he was related to any path to civilization. On three occasions, his route included small hollows although none with fresh water. Once, a rabbit loped across such a basin, but no other game appeared. He was sweating from the near noon heat and he thought about the night and the before-dawn chill that had stiffened his joints.

He smelled coffee!

The arroyo led into another open place and Tom stopped. Directly ahead of him, a torn square of canvas was tented on four poles over the entrance to a mineshaft. On the ground nearby, a small campfire flickered under a metal stand with a coffeepot on top. Nearby, a mule was tethered to a fir tree.

Tom heard the cocking of a pistol behind him and raised both hands.

"Whatcha doing here, mister?"

"Can I turn around?"

"No, sir. Keep those hands up high 'til I get your side arm."

"I'd rather you'd not."

"I'll do it anyway. You standing still or laying still."

Tom's sidewise gaze saw the dark hand pluck the Colt from his holster and heard the man back away.

"You can turn now."

Tom turned slowly with hands remaining high. The man was tall, six feet and an inch or two more, well built and smooth muscled. His color was walnut rather than mahogany, a mature and nearly handsome face crowned with close-cropped white hair. His clothing was a pair of denim trousers and work shirt, both in good shape, white socks and black shoes on his feet.

"You want a cup of coffee?" the man asked.

"I'd appreciate it," Tom replied.

"While we talk, I'd like an answer."

"About what I'm doing here?"

"Yes, sir. Step over to my living place and we'll talk."

The man walked behind Tom at a ten-foot distance as they moved to the makeshift awning. "Sit in the shade if you've a mind for the comfort," he said. "No chairs, but make yourself comfortable."

"You don't talk like a field hand," Tom said.

"I was a houseman. Damned Yankees lost me my good wife and my young son and God knows where they ever got to. Had a good life, but damned Yankees had to make me free and ruin it all." He waited while

Tom sat on the ground just under the edge of the canvas. "Now, what are you doing out here?"

"Running from something you likely won't believe."

"Try me."

"I spent the night at a ranch back on the Placerville road. Woke up when I heard gunshots. There were two fellows laying in the yard, one hurt and one dead. Then, another was gunned down and, after that, a half dozen men started shooting at me saying *I* was the one who done the killing." He paused. "I went on the run, shinnied myself up a mountain and been wandering here for . . . this is my second day."

"You're right. I don't believe you."

"Didn't think you would." Tom paused. "How about that coffee?"

"There's a cup right there by the stove. Only got the one cup. Bother you I've been drinking from it?"

Tom crawled cautiously to the stove, found the cup and filled it. He crawled back under the awning and took a tentative sip. "Damned hot . . . but damned good."

"Had anything to eat?"

Tom shook his head.

"Already had my breakfast and wasn't planning on something for noon. Can you wait 'til supper?"

"Fine. Can I ask you a question?"

The Negro nodded.

"What are you doing out here? This your claim?"

"Maybe. Maybe a dry hole and just place for me to stay out of the weather."

"None of my business and I ain't claim jumping. If you'll just point me the way outta these hills and I'll be on my way."

"Probably should've shot you but I do like having some company. Gets lonely here, only me and the critters. You got a name so we can talk?

"Tom Patterson. Yours?"

"Isaiah Washington. They call me Ike."

"How'd they get the Ike sound out of Isaiah?"

His host shrugged.

They talked for two hours as the sun arced across the sky until it hid behind the neighboring bluffs. As they talked, tensions eased. "I'm beginning to take a liking to you, Tom," Ike said at last. "And maybe I'll take to believing that story you gave me."

"Like me enough to give my gun back?"

"Like you okay. Didn't say anything yet about trusting you."

Tom brought the pepperbox out of his pocket.

Ike smiled. "Had that on me all the while?"

Tom nodded.

Reaching behind his back, Ike retrieved the Colt revolver and handed it to Tom. "Let's fix an early supper."

Supper included fried bacon and corn meal mush, a can of baked beans and another pot of coffee. Still at a distance, they ate their meals from tin plates, one a spare that Ike found after much rummaging. They shared the cup.

"Spend the night if you'd like, Tom," Ike proposed.

"If those people out there are hunting for you, a couple of days camping here might make 'em give up and go home."

"Think I'll rob you during your sleep?"

"Well, I don't have any gold dust and nothing here's worth stealing except Buster, that mule of mine. You try to make off with Buster and he won't budge unless he wants to. Even me, I can't always make him go."

"I'm kinda dumb about mules . . . you call him *him*?"

"I don't call him *it*."

They laughed.

"You stay inside the mine?" Tom asked and gestured to the cavity in the rock wall.

Ike nodded. "Front part of it. I got a couple of blankets in there, one I'll give you. Nights get a little nippy, but not bad at all."

Tom gave a wide smile. "Best offer of the day. I thank you indeed."

Chapter Thirteen

Betty Patterson leaned on her forearms across the top rail of the corral and watched as Uncle Willie and George Martinez finished hitching the two draft horses to the high-wheeled, long wagon at the side of the livery stable. Uncle Willie had come with the deal when Tom and Betty had purchased the freight business, the Belgian horses and rolling stock equipment from Bert Stevens, the semi-retired owner. George, with family on either side of the California and Mexican border, had been their staff addition. He was a strong and sturdy young man not yet twenty-three with a smart, handsome head on his shoulders and always reliable at work and at home.

Tom and Betty paid to share the use of the large barn and corral with Stevens, who continued to operate a buggy and buckboard rental business out of the same building.

"Getting too old for the heavy lifting," Stevens had told them at the transfer of business. "Appreciate it if you'd keep Uncle Willie on. He's a little simpleminded, but he's steady and strong for a man pushing sixty. He'll do what you tell him and you can count on him."

Betty smiled as she watched her two employees as they talked and prepared for their journey. Uncle Willie was giving instructions, thinking he was in charge and the young man pretended he was. They were ready to move out for a short run to pick up and deliver an over-sized load of bricks from the lumberyard to a building site south of town. She continued to watch as Uncle Willie drove the huge wagon out of the compound with George signaling clearances as the rig moved from the barn onto the street.

"Pardon, Mrs. Patterson."

She turned to see Marshal Judd behind her. "Marshal," she responded. "Can I help you?"

The lawman shifted his considerable weight from side to side, obviously discomfited at his mission. "There's a problem, ma'am. Ain't no way to say it . . ."

"Just say it, Marshal."

"I got a wire from the sheriff down in El Dorado County. Your husband did something bad down near there."

Betty waited for him to continue.

"Shot and killed one man and then beat another poor old fellow to death. Cold-blooded murder, they say."

Betty took a long, tremulous breath. "Is he in jail?"

"No, ma'am. He got away and he's hiding out somewhere in them mountains. Lots of men looking for him."

"Whatever Tom did or didn't do, it wouldn't be murder," Betty said, a hard edge in her voice. "It would be self-defense if there was a shooting and Tom wouldn't ever beat someone to death, especially an old man."

"Facts seem to be otherwise, ma'am."

"You think he's here?"

The fat man shrugged. "Probably not yet, but I came by to warn you not to hide him or give him any help. If he does show, you tell him to give himself up."

Betty gave a smile of contempt. "I'll surely do that, Marshal."

The lawman scowled at the scorn in her voice. "For your own good, ma'am. I'm doing my duty and I'll bring charges against you same as him, you do anything to help him."

"Waddle back down to your jail, Marshal. Tom can take care of himself and if he needs my help, he'll get it with or without your warnings."

"You and him are a smart aleck bunch. Just 'cause you're a woman don't think I won't slap the—"

"Land's sake, I do think I could handle you by myself," she cut in with a disdainful laugh. Without waiting for a response, she turned her back to him and walked to the barn. He was swearing loudly, the exact words ignored by her as she entered the barn. She moved to an open door on the front side of the tack room and walked inside.

Bert sat drowsing in a swivel chair at a rolltop desk, his feet propped up on an opened lower desk drawer.

"Bert!"

The old man blinked and came fully awake, his feet dropping to the floor as he turned the chair to face her. "Howdy, Miss Betty. You need me?"

She nodded. "I do need your help, Bert. I've got to go out of town for a spell . . . don't know exactly how long. Can I ask you to fill in and run the business for us 'til we get home?"

The old man smiled broadly, showing space-gapped teeth. "Done it before, lady," he reminded her. "Be happy to do you a turn."

"I know that, Bert. We'll share the profits for any business while we're gone as we've done in the past."

"I'll take good care of everything. Where you heading?"

"Down around Placerville. I'd appreciate it if nobody else knows, especially that no good Marshal Judd."

"I'll keep it to myself, ma'am," he said with a nod. "When you leaving?"

"As soon as I pack a few things. Then I'll be on my way."

Langdon Sherwood drummed his fingers on the arm of his chair as Carl Parrish recounted the events at the Porter ranch.

"Not exactly as we planned, but it'll work itself out just fine," the big man said as he finished.

"I still don't like it," the lawyer complained. "As long as he's alive, he can tell his side of the story . . . and there may be some who'll believe him."

"He'll be shot on sight," Parrish countered. "Manhunt going on all through California, Nevada and parts thereabouts."

The two men were seated in the antechamber of an upstairs bedroom suite in a Placerville hotel. Sherwood had arrived on the train from Sacramento and checked in to await Parrish's arrival in the late afternoon.

"What about young Porter?" Sherwood asked.

"All riled up about his old man," Parrish replied. "Kid puts on one hell of an act. You'd think he really gave a damn about his pa. He's pushing the law hard on going into the back country after Patterson."

"Don't let him overdo it," Sherwood advised.

"Kept bracing the county sheriff," Parrish admitted. "I told him to back off."

"Any problems with the sheriff?"

Parrish was slow in responding. "I don't think so, but he ain't no dummy."

The lawyer gave a sigh. "Carl, you say things are working out but I'll tell you I'm not impressed with what you've done so far."

"Getting Patterson was your idea in the first place," Parrish said defensively. "So the Central Pacific wouldn't be suspected."

"I concede your point. I thought it better to have it appear a grudge killing than to draw attention to any business interests that would benefit." He paused, then continued, "Central Pacific is not involved, never was, never will be. It's not in their interest to compete with the main line running through Reno down to Auburn." The small man lifted his hands, palms up. "I'm no longer associated with that railroad. This is a brand new enterprise, an independent rail venture financed by important men who can see the enormous potential."

"Too bad old man Porter . . . or Portee, that is, wouldn't sell."

"He came home from the war a marked man," Sherwood said. "Cashiered from the army, disgraced . . . his family had once been important in this area. He even changed his name hoping the world and folks hereabouts would forget." He smirked. "He became a recluse in that house, clinging to his property with some sort of a crazy thought that if he stayed there, it would make everything right again."

"Can't reason with a crazy man," Parrish agreed. "Saved us all a lot of trouble if he'd listened." He shrugged. "It *is* going to be okay, Mr. Sherwood," the large man persisted. "Look at it this way . . . if I hadn't threatened Patterson's wife, he would've had no call to come looking for me."

Sherwood gave the statement considerable contemplation and, finally, shrugged. "Let's hope it is okay, Carl. Not only our fortunes are at risk but our very lives as well. Stay after Patterson 'til he's dead and out of the way." He gave an impatient wave of his hand. "Keep me informed."

"Just as you say, sir." Parrish rose and left the room.

Five minutes later, there was a soft knock at the door.

"Come in!" Sherwood called.

The door opened and a balding, middle-aged man walked in.

"Afternoon, John."

John Driscoll crossed the room and seated himself. "I saw your man leave," the newspaper editor said. "Everything all right?"

Sherwood nodded. "I think so. They missed killing Patterson but they've got him on the run. With the publicity of a manhunt, it might make an even better story. It's up to you and others to ensure there's a public outcry against him."

"I didn't know there was going to be killing," Driscoll complained.

Sherwood gave a derisive grunt. "Well, you're part and parcel of it, so don't get cold feet now. Stay in the buggy and we'll all be rich."

"I'll do what I can, Langdon. You were right that he might be coming to see me. I told him about Parrish, where he had to be and I headed him in the right direction." He paused in thought and shook his head. "Still, I'd be extremely wary of this man. There's something about him that I . . ." He shook his head again, not finishing his statement.

"You do your job, we'll do ours," Sherwood told him. "He's one man against whatever resources or how many men we need to destroy him. He hasn't got a chance."

"I hope you're right," the editor said solemnly. "Until he's out of things for sure, I've got this uneasy feeling."

Chapter Fourteen

"Any idea of how I can get out of here?" Tom asked.

The two men were sitting cross-legged on the ground in the shade of the canvas awning.

"Won't be easy," Ike said. "Been thinking on that."

"And?"

"Did have some sort of a crazy idea."

"Let's hear it."

"Ever been to a minstrel show?"

"Saw one once."

"White men put black on their faces and make silly jokes and pretending they're really stupid colored folks."

"What'cha getting at?"

"I come and go in these mountains and folks are used to seeing me," Ike told him. "Travel up and down the road when I go for supplies."

"Hell, that ain't going to work!" Tom said, although a wide grin appeared as he guessed what Ike had in mind.

"Hear me out. You and me, we're not much different in size. What we do is burn us some dead trees, smear some burnt ashes all over your face, neck and hands, put you in my hat and my clothes and—"

"It ain't going to work, Ike."

"And I'll loan you Buster," Ike resumed. "You come out on the road right around sundown. People see you walking along with my mule, thinking it's me, and you'll likely get clear."

"Ike, you can't loan me your mule! It wouldn't be right."

"You get clear and you make it right, whatever it's worth to you whenever you please," Ike said, then added, "You may wonder why."

Tom nodded.

"It's true, I'm prospecting, but I live in here 'cause it's safer for me. Tried living in town for a while and some fellow claimed I said something bad to a white woman. It wasn't true, but folks thought it just the same." He paused. "I know how it is not to be believed."

Tom didn't respond for a few minutes. "If I was to do this fool thing, how'd I get Buster to move?"

"There's a trick to it. I carry a little switch and just tap him a couple of times just under his left front leg. Don't know why, but it usually moves him right along." He stood up. "Come on, let me show you how."

* * *

"You got about an hour of daylight left. It's four miles going up and down that way to the main road. Even so, it's a pretty easy walk." Ike chuckled. "If I look as bad as you, no wonder they wouldn't want me in town."

Tom's face was grungy gray with soot, Ike's battered, tall crowned hat pulled low on his head, a red bandanna round his neck and a ragged poncho over his own shirt and jeans. He held Buster's halter lead in his left hand and carried a switch in the other.

"Keep your head bowed down when you meet people on the road," Ike advised. "That's what colored folks are supposed to do. Don't ever make eye contact with anyone and don't say much if and when someone talks to you. Just nod and say yah, sah or naw, sah like I always do. Which way you heading?"

"The man I'm after I reckon was heading back toward Placerville," Tom replied. "Might as well follow and see if I can't turn him in when I tell my side of things." He gestured to the mule. "If I get clear, what'll I do with Buster?"

"Hitch him first place you feel safe along the road. I'll come find him and fetch him home in the morning. Good luck."

Tom led Buster onto the road as twilight rendered the color of the landscape to muted shades. As far as he could see, in either direction, the road was empty of traffic. He gently tapped the balky mule into motion and set off at a meandering pace toward Placerville.

A half-hour and two miles later, two men on horse-back came up behind him.

"Hey, Ike!" shouted one. "Where you going this time of evening?"

Tom lifted a hand to point down the road.

The rider who spoke spurred his horse in front of Tom and blocked his way. Tom kept his face angled toward the ground and stood still.

"You hear me, boy?"

"Yah, suh," Tom said in a voice he hoped sounded like Ike's.

"You ain't Ike!" the rider accused.

"No, suh," Tom said huskily. "His cousin. Jes' vissin'."

"You see anybody on the road or back in them hills?"

"No, suh."

"There's a dangerous man roaming around. You'd tell me if you'd really seen him, wouldn't you?"

"Yah, suh, I surely would."

"You see him, you be careful of him," the rider cautioned and spurred his horse to the side of the road. "You best hurry on if you want to get to Bulie's store before it closes."

Tom nodded and applied the switch behind Buster's left front leg. He and the mule moved again at the animal's unhurried pace. Tom didn't turn around to see, but he gave a ragged sigh of relief as he heard the patrolling pair turn their horses and trot back the way they'd come.

Night fell as Tom and Buster continued their journey. From time to time, scattered clouds darkened the landscape as they drifted across the quarter moon. Tom pondered what to do. What few wagons still traveled this thoroughfare would not move through the night and daylight would give him little chance to sneak unseen into the back of a wagon. He considered the thought of stealing a horse, but it would likely involve gunplay with innocents and that was not an option. He could walk on in the flimsy guise of a colored man and his mule and hope no other riders would intercept and examine him closely. *No other choice. Push on and pray.*

After another mile, he came to a long, narrow frame building where lantern light shone through the front window. From what he could see through the glass panes, the front part of the structure housed a counter with shelves on the wall, behind it displaying a meager supply of various canned goods. He saw a shadow of someone moving in the store and then caught a glimpse of an older man entering an interior hallway. The back part of the building was likely the living quarters for the storekeeper and his family. *Bulie's place*, Tom decided.

Out of consideration for Ike's convenience, he thought about leaving Buster tied near the building. He discarded the thought immediately; he was not yet far enough away from the prime search area where men were hunting for him.

Estimating the time near midnight, Tom led the mule to a hitching rail in front of another building, a small, dark shack. Occupied or not, it made better sense to leave Buster where he *might* belong rather than leave him conspicuously tied to a tree beside the road. Tom gave the mule an affectionate pat on the rump and resumed his walk toward Placerville.

The night was still with only the sounds of a gentle wind to softly rustle the trees and the occasional cries of wild things in the hills on either side of the road. The earlier clouds had wafted from the sky and left it clear for moon and star shine. In spite of his plight or, perhaps because of it, Tom felt a sense of serenity, a reverential accord with the universe. *Lucky to be alive and lucky to have made it this far, God knows how.*

Hour after hour, he trudged on. No wagons or riders appeared; the patrols more than likely left far behind. As he walked, he mulled over what he could do if he made it to the town. The manhunt would apt to be concentrated in any nearby settlements and would intensify should the law suspect he had escaped from the mountains. *Even if I catch up with Parrish, what good would it do? A forced confession? How likely would that be and who'd believe it?*

As the pre-dawn light began to diffuse the starlit sky, Tom saw a large, dark shape emerge from a thick grove of trees and lumber across the road sixty feet ahead. He stopped and stood still, dismayed to feel the gentle breeze behind him. *I'm upwind, damn it!*

Even in the faint light, he could see the distinctive

white-tipped long hairs on the animal's back and the hump behind the animal's head. *Grizzly!*

The horrendous bear stopped moving and raised its muzzle to catch the scent. With a roar, it reared on hind legs to a height of seven, perhaps, eight feet.

Tom drew his Colt and waited.

The bear dropped to all fours and advanced for a yard, then three, then five. Again, it reared and gave a fearsome roar.

Tom stood very still and slowly raised his arm to aim the revolver. *How many to stop him? Five in the chambers! Thank God I reloaded!*

The grizzly continued to growl and rumble its fierce challenge and, on hind legs, moved forward and stopped again.

Tom took a slow backward step, never taking his eyes from the bear, then stepped back again, a twig snapping under his boot.

The grizzly roared at the sound, attention fixed upon Tom. Dropping down, the bear made a fearsome charge, bellowing fury. It loped toward Tom coming within twenty feet and, again, the beast reared to full height, baring sharp teeth, raking the air with the long claws of both paws.

Tom stood very still, his revolver pointed directly at the animal's head. *In the eyes! Empty it, now! Don't wait for the charge! Every shot into the damned thing's brain!*

The grizzly's roar receded to a guttural growl.

Tom held his rigid pose and did not fire.

The bear continued its snarling discontent for two dreadful minutes more, then dropped to its forelegs and silently entered a wooded glade on the other side of the road.

Shaken and trembling, Tom moved slowly to the side of the road to the trunk of a substantial cottonwood and stepped behind it. He remained behind the tree for a long time, watchful. He had seen bears before at a long distance, but never one this dangerous and this close. With a tremulous sigh of relief, still with his Colt at the ready, he stepped out to the road and warily walked past the place where he had last seen the predator. He walked a little faster once past that location, glad to see the woodland give way to an open landscape.

"Forgot about bears," he muttered in guilt. "Hope that one don't find Buster."

With the sun breaking over the horizon, he hurried on.

Chapter Fifteen

Late in the afternoon, Betty checked into a hotel in Placerville and made arrangements for a livery stable to care for her horse and buggy. Dusty from the trip, she bathed, changed into a fresh, modest dress and came downstairs from her room for an early evening meal in the hotel dining room. Seated alone at a white-cloth table, she was aware of the bold looks of solitary men and even the occasional furtive glances of those dining with female companions. The women in the room regarded her closely and suspiciously, envious of her beauty. Ignoring all, she ordered a light supper that included a salad, a small cut of beef and garden vegetables.

After supper, she picked up a copy of the local paper at the hotel desk and found a chair out in the evening cool of the hotel's veranda. The front page of the *Placerville Weekly Press* featured a banner headline: KILLER AT LARGE! The sub-headline identified Tom Patterson as a dangerous and coldhearted killer. The lead article described the murders at the Porter ranch. An interview with the son of the slain rancher, Jedidiah Porter, detailed the bad blood between the two men resulting from a wartime encounter. The slant of the news article painted the elder Porter as an innocent in the Civil War conflict and Tom as the aggressor. It further identified the latter as a notorious and bloodthirsty gunman, the harsh accusation demonstrated by the brutal slaying of the elderly ranch hand, Zeke Hamilton.

Sighing her contempt, she turned to an inside page to finish the article. On the back page, she found a full-page notice offering a $2,000 reward for the capture or, preferably, the death of her husband.

One of the lone men from the dining room strolled out onto the porch and pretended to look at the evening scene of the town. Well dressed, handsome in his early forties with a pompadour of copious brown hair brushed high above his forehead, he was seemingly vain despite his noticeably overweight body. He made no effort to conceal his audacious glances at Betty, hoping to catch her eye and initiate conversation.

"Do you have a match?" she asked.

The man smiled showing his confidence. He took a gold case from his pocket and opened it to display slender cheroots. "May I offer you one of mine? From Havana."

"No, but I do need the match."

He nodded, reached in his pocket and took out a small box of matches. He offered it to her.

"Would you light one for me, please?"

The man nodded again, took out a single match and scratched the head on the side of the box.

The match flared.

"Thank you," she said and touched the bottom of the newspaper to the flame. She held it as it burned into a torch and tossed it over the banister.

"Something in the paper you didn't like?"

She nodded.

"Anything else I can do for you?"

She slowly shook her head and started for the door. The man reached for and caught her arm.

Betty jerked her arm away and drew the hilt of stiletto from the cuff of her sleeve, displaying part of a glittering blade. "Rooster, touch me again and you're a capon."

The man took a step back.

"Thanks for the match," she said. "Good evening."

Tom guessed the time was well past midnight. He had spent the daylight hours in hiding well off the road and, when the sun was low in the sky, he had walked to a small creek and knelt beside the cascading stream. Only a couple of miles from Placerville, it had been time to wash off all traces of what was left of his imperfect disguise. He had stripped and splashed the cold water over his face and body to rinse away the residue of ashes. Then, he sat on the bank and soaked his aching feet in the flowing stream. He had hidden Ike's poncho under a patch of scrub brush, retained the weather-beaten hat and then returned to sit and wait beside the stream.

Now, he walked back to the road and hiked the short distance into the town. The streets were empty with a negligible number of overhead lanterns to provide a minimum illumination. Almost all of the houses and buildings were dark; oil lamps shone from windows of a very few indicating people that were up very early or quite late. There were few sounds; an occasional sigh of wind as it swirled through the town, the sporadic barking of a distant dog and, once, a muffled and unintelligible male shout from inside some indeterminate dwelling.

He kept to the murky shadows of the buildings cast by the faint moonlight, staying on the hard pan at the edge of the central street. He avoided the boardwalk, concerned the pressure of his steps might creak a plank or two and awaken a light sleeper. He moved into a greater darkness between two buildings to hide from any night owl's inadvertent view.

Well, I'm here . . . what the hell do I do now?

Getting to civilization, no matter what the risks, was the only way he could set things right. He considered surrendering to the law and, indecisive about it, rejected that option for the time being. To clear himself, he hoped to find Parrish as a first step in solving the puzzle of his predicament.

Tom studied the empty street, his eyes searching the silent buildings. In a few hours, this central avenue would be teeming with traffic, tradesmen, retailers and customers flowing in and out of the business district, buying and selling. If Parrish was still in town, chances are he had to show up on this main street. Tom realized a need not only for a place of hiding, but a high vantage where he could survey the entire area. He scanned the dark street, looking for an empty building with an upstairs window.

None there.

Another possibility came to mind: He concentrated on the rooftops and found a suitable choice in a two-story building across the street. It appeared to be of a flat-roofed design topped with a large painted wooden sign, THE BOLTON BUILDING, extended above the front roof's edge. The lower part of the building housed a furniture store and a second-story entry door was accessible by an outside stairway.

Tom looked right and left, then walked across the road to the side of the building, glancing to make sure he had not been seen. At the foot of the steps, a plaque on the sidewall listed four private offices on the upper level—two lawyers, a doctor and a dentist. Tom eased up the flight of steps to the upper banistered landing and paused, seeking some approach to the roof. Four feet away, multiple iron straps bound a drainpipe to the structure's corner wall.

"More damned climbing," he said. He went over the railing and held to it as he leaned out and stretched his right hand for one of the straps. He curled his fingers over it and swung his body to the pipe, his left hand on the other side of the strap.

There was a slight sound as a nail squeaked an inch out of the pine siding.

No time to dawdle. Trying to make as little noise as he could, he began to shinny up the drainpipe. Hand over hand, he pulled himself up, relying mostly on the strength of his arms while clamping his knees tight against the pipe to hold his position each time he reached higher.

At the top of the downspout, he lunged for the overhanging roof eave and pulled himself over it. He rested for two minutes and then crept along the edge to the front side of the building, then moved to the building center and squatted down behind the large sign. On either side of this building, other rooftops were lower. Only one of similar height at some distance away might have afforded some person a line of sight to his position. From his position, by peering around each end of the sign, he would be able to command a bird's-eye view of the street and those who traveled it.

Satisfied, Tom sat behind the sign and leaned back against the roof edge wall and closed his eyes.

Chapter Sixteen

"**I**'d like to speak with the sheriff."

Across the large front office of the jailhouse where he shared space with his three deputies, Sheriff Willis Morgan looked up from his deskwork, his interest captured by the woman's mellifluous voice.

"I'll handle it, Nick," Morgan called to the burly deputy sitting at a desk positioned near the gate of the waist-high slatted railing that separated the entry space from the office area of the facility. The sheriff walked to the railing gate and nodded his chief deputy back to work. He glanced meaningfully at the two other deputies standing at the rifle rack who were ogling the attractive woman. Instantly, they resumed a serious interest in the weapons they were cleaning. "I'm Sheriff Morgan. How may I help you, ma'am?"

"I'm Mrs. Patterson. Mrs. Tom Patterson."

The sheriff's eyebrows lifted and he nodded. "Mrs. Patterson."

"Is there somewhere we can talk?"

Again, he nodded and opened the gate. "I have a room." He ushered her along a short corridor and, before they reached the barred jail cell entry, he opened a side door into a windowless room. "I hope this will do."

Betty walked in and noted the small table and three chairs. There was no other furniture in the room and nothing on the walls. "This is where you question prisoners?"

"Yes, ma'am. Like I said, I hope this will do. We don't have no private offices." He pulled one of the chairs back from the table and Betty sank onto it. "I 'spect you want to talk about your husband."

"Yes, sir. He hasn't been shot or hurt in any way?"

Morgan shook his head. "Still at large."

"I've read the newspaper story and, I tell you, every word of it . . . it's not true."

"Seems to be, ma'am."

"Do you know anything about my husband?"

Morgan settled into a chair across from her. "Yes, as a matter-of-fact, I do know the name. I know he was a lawman and a good one from what I hear."

"He enforced the law . . . he didn't break it."

The sheriff frowned. "Begging your pardon, Mrs. Patterson, but I've heard that there *were* a few times early on."

"He had a past, I'll admit. I suspect most of you did." She smiled. "I asked a couple of questions around town about you."

Morgan laughed, then sobered. "I'll grant you that, ma'am. However, setting aside some hard opinions and the way words was said, that newspaper account has it just about right. The dead man's son and another ranch hand were witnesses and swore to it. Young Jed Porter said your husband came looking for his pa over some bad feelings what happened back in the war."

Betty shook her head vehemently. "Sheriff, I've heard some parts of that war story from Tom and, believe me, he'd put that behind him. What he felt about that terrible man, that was the past and he'd left it there for good."

"Then *why* was he here?" Morgan's tone was skeptical.

"Tom was here looking for a man, but it wasn't for anyone named Porter."

"And who might that man be?"

"A man who called himself Patrick Mahoney. We doubt that's his real name. Hotel clerk up in Auburn said this Mahoney had been seen in these parts. And that's why Tom was here, he was looking for that man."

"What did Mr. Patterson want with this, as you call him, Mahoney fellow?"

"Like I said, we don't think that's his real name. Whoever he is, he came looking for Tom and wanted to hire him to kill somebody. Tom told him straight out he would have nothing to do with that sort of thing."

"Maybe he changed his mind."

Anger flashed in Betty's face. "No, sir. He's no hired killer. Those same danged people even tried to kidnap me to make Tom do what they wanted."

After a long, thoughtful pause, the lawman sighed. "You're not exactly what I'd call an impartial woman." He gave her an apologetic look. "See here, Mrs. Patterson, I appreciate your thinking good of your husband. It's what I'd expect a loyal wife to do. I try to be a fair man and I know I've only heard the one side of it. It sure don't look good for your mister, but I'll try not to be the judge and jury on this. If he gets in touch with you, you tell him to give himself up to me and I'll see to it that he gets a fair shake."

"What good will it do for him to be in a jail with no way to prove he's innocent?"

"We can recommend a good lawyer—"

"There's something funny going on, Sheriff," Betty interrupted. "Something you and all the rest ain't seeing. I'd check those so called witnesses and hammer 'em good to make them tell the real story."

"I'll do my best, ma'am," the sheriff said, rising from his chair. "Best you go on back home and give me some time to look things over."

Betty rose. "Just go home and let people hunt Tom down?"

"Best not interfere, ma'am."

They left the room and walked to the front door of

the jail where the lawman opened the door and glanced at the sky. "Best hurry, ma'am. Looks like we're going to have a storm."

As Betty gave him a wan smile and walked out, the sheriff closed the door and turned to his senior deputy at his desk nearby. "There *is* something fishy about this whole thing, Nick."

The deputy, a broad-shouldered law officer in his late thirties, looked up, a question in his expression.

"Hell, I don't know what it is." Morgan sighed. "It's just a feeling like she said. Something we just ain't seeing."

Thunder muttered as the storm approached from the Pacific coast. Tom eyed the billowing clouds with some consternation not only for the probable downpour, but also because of the numerous and ominous streaks of lightning.

"Gonna be soaking wet and likely to get lightning struck to boot," he said aloud. He turned back to peer around the sign at the street below. It had been a hot morning, the heat intensified by the black tar roofing surface surrounding him and nothing had come of his surveillance. Parrish had not appeared and his miserable observation post seemed a waste. Other than a questionable place to hide, the rooftop—first a place for broiling and now a site for drenching rain and thunderbolts—didn't seem worth the effort. Once again,

Tom felt the urge to climb down and surrender. *At least I'd be out of the weather in a nice dry cell.*

A few minutes later, the first drops of rain spattered the roof and then intensified into a deluge. Thunder boomed and lightning ripped through the purple skies. Tom huddled against the sign for what little shielding it might provide from the sheeting rain. However, in less than thirty seconds he was completely drenched.

The downpour continued for nearly an hour, diminished to a drizzle and finally came to a dripping end. The thunderheads were moving over the Sierra Nevada Mountains and the sun shone intermittently through the rifts of the clouds.

Wet, cold and shivering, Tom eased on his knees to the right edge of the sign and looked down into the street. People were beginning to emerge from the stores and buildings, men and an occasional woman tiptoeing through the mud in the main street. After the storm, men on horseback, buggies and wagons moved slowly along the boggy avenue, the commerce of the town resuming. At first, he could see nothing other than a repeat of the earlier hours, no sign of Parrish or the other men who'd pursued him at the ranch.

He was about to move to the other side of the sign when something caught his eye. Down the street at some distance, several horses were tied at the rail of a saloon. One horse, in the midst of a cluster of others, looked very much like his own. He focused his sight on the animal's color and the star marking on the head, then studied the saddle and saddlebags.

"Ginger, by heavens!" Tom exclaimed. "Damnation, some thief is riding my horse."

Chapter Seventeen

Jed Porter sat at a table in the Good Times Saloon with two unkempt young men of his same age. All three seemed uncomfortable and unaccustomed to the ill-fitting suits they were wearing. Their soiled linen collars were detached and set aside along with their dirty wrinkled ties. Half-finished beer mugs sat on top of the table in front of Jed's friends. Jed swigged the last of his beer and thumped the schooner on the table beside the empty shot glass.

"It was a nice funeral for your old man," one young man, Dave, said for a third time. "Preacher did a good job."

The other young man, Bobby, nodded agreement.

"Well, it's over and done," Jed philosophized. "Glad

we got him covered up before the rain came down." He raised his empty shot glass to the bartender behind the pine wood bar across the room.

The bartender nodded and turned to the bottles arrayed on the back bar.

"How's it feel now to own your own place?" Bobby asked.

"Ain't really thought about it," Jed replied and turned a bright smile to the barmaid as she approached the table and placed whiskey and a beer on the table. "Thank you, hon," he said. "I'll settle up before we leave."

The young woman gave him a feigned smile and walked away.

"Better looking than some of the others," Dave ventured. "Lord knows where they come from."

"All parts," Bobby gave his opinion. "They ain't the brightest in the world."

"Dorie's all right," Jed said. "She ain't so dumb. Bet she makes more money in tips from drunk cowhands every week than you two in a month."

"Whatcha going to do now?" Dave asked.

"Haven't given it all that much thinking," Jed replied. "Maybe I'll run the ranch, make some improvements . . . or maybe I'll sell it and get outta this damned hole in the wall. Sell it and move over to San Francisco and live the sporting life."

Dave hooted. "Who'd buy that place?"

"You'd be surprised," Jed responded, annoyance in his voice.

"That just talk or you got somebody interested?" Dave persisted.

"None of your business, Davey."

"Sorry. Just passing the time."

"You got a new horse out there, Jed?" Bobby asked. "Ain't seen you on that one before."

"Belonged to the murderer that shot my old man."

"What's going on with that?" Dave asked. "Any wind of him?"

Jed shook his head. "I wanted to go into the back-country after him. That fool sheriff wouldn't hear of it. He ain't much of a lawman. Probably afraid Patterson would shoot him dead."

"Is it you putting up that reward?" Bobby asked.

"I ain't putting up no two thousand dollars, newspaper folks, I guess. Whole damned county is looking for him. I don't see no need for me or nobody else to spend good money for the law to do what they're supposed to do."

"He's been gone awhile," Dave said. "What happens if he gets away?"

"That ain't likely. If he don't die out there starving to death or getting ate by a mountain lion, he'll come out and be shot on sight."

"Maybe they'll take him alive,"

"Not if I have anything to do with it," Jed said and gulped down his whiskey and looked across the room. "Hey, Dorie!"

Langdon Sherwood removed the pince-nez from his

eyes and polished each lens with a handkerchief and then peered at the small group of men in his hotel suite. Parrish, immaculately attired for the occasion, was leaning against the back wall, occasionally shifting his attention out the window to observe the receding rain clouds. Three expensively dressed men were seated, two in a settee and a much older gentleman in a chair. In appearance, they were businessmen of obvious importance, but the diminutive lawyer's manner of confidence dominated the group. Off to the side in a corner, the newspaper editor, Driscoll, shifted uneasily in his chair as Sherwood resumed his discourse.

"As I was saying," Sherwood resumed, "there is no need for your concern. The death of Edward Porter was a tragic matter of propitious chance. An old rebel enemy with a grudge from back in the war came looking for the poor man and killed him. That criminal is still at large, on the run with the entire state of California on the hunt for him. It is only a matter of time before he is caught and brought to justice." He paused, a glance at Driscoll arrested the newsman's fidgeting. "However, as the saying goes, 'tis an ill wind that blows nobody good.' It *is* to our good fortune that Porter's property, which he absolutely refused to sell for a number of rather foolish reasons, may now be a viable prospect."

"Have you talked to the son?" a jowly gray-haired man on the settee questioned. Seated at his right, the other man on the settee, middle-aged and balding, nodded his agreeing interest.

"Not yet," Sherwood replied. "A little too soon since the funeral was just this morning."

"What makes you think he'll be different than his father?" asked the bald man.

"The young man has expressed a view that he'd like to leave this area and move to a more exciting locale."

"When this venture was first proposed, nothing was said of right-of-way problems," the elderly businessman in the chair stated. "Why weren't we told of it sooner?"

"Because we were confident that we would be able to solve any difficulties," Sherwood assured him. "We were sure that Porter would've come around."

"This death seems awfully convenient," the bald man said.

"A coincidence," Sherwood said smoothly. "Nothing more."

"What if this hadn't happened and he wouldn't sell?" came the question from the old man in the chair.

"Eminent domain. A lengthy government procedure, but we could've taken the property through the courts."

"Not necessarily," the bald man scoffed. "Not with all the bad publicity railroads have been getting. Ever since that Mussel Slough shooting affair last May, hired killers shooting farmers for their land . . . the courts might just as well toss it out and then where would we be?"

"But that hasn't happened in this case nor will it," Sherwood said crisply. "We are confident in our ability to purchase the land from young Porter. Your investments are safe and secure. What moneys you've put in and what you will further invest will bring all of you fortunes beyond your comprehension. I've been in touch with eastern financial firms and a number are eager to finalize the issuance of the necessary bonds."

"We don't want to get mixed up in anything off color," the old man said. "We got a name for this railroad yet?"

Sherwood did not comment.

"You'll let us know?" the man of drooping cheeks inquired.

"Of course. Now, gentlemen, shall we repair to the dining room for an early supper?"

Betty sat on a chair by the window in her room, her mood as gloomy as the squally weather. Her trip to Placerville had been a futile and foolish waste; there was nothing further she could do. The sheriff had been polite and seemingly sincere, but she knew his assurances of just actions were of little merit. Chances were Tom would be a target rather than a captive.

Even in her despair, there was a hope that Tom would, in some mystical way, sense her presence in the area and find her. It was her wild and impractical wish that she could help him, to spirit him out of this danger. *Not likely.*

Tomorrow, she decided with reluctance, she would head home to Red Cliff and pray that, somehow, Tom could get out of this area and come to her. She shook her head, stood and walked to the door. *Get out of this wretched room!*

She opened the door and took a step into the upper corridor and paused as she saw the group of men a few feet ahead. At the top of the stairway, they turned and started down the steps to the hotel lobby.

Betty stifled a gasp and stepped back into the shadowed doorframe. Leading the descending group—the lawyer, Langdon Sherwood! And right behind him, a large, black-bearded man with a scar on his face and a silk cravat at his throat! *The very man Tom was seeking?*

Betty moved back into her room, her despondency replaced with a fervent enlightenment and a fierce anger.

That dirty, double-dealing crook! I was right to come after all!

Two hours after sundown, Tom lowered himself over the eave and trusted his weight to the drainpipe once again. He moved all the way down to the ground hopeful the outside stairway would screen his descent from any occasional passersby. He walked from between the two buildings and moved along the boardwalk, hoping a casual manner would not draw attention.

There were only a few men on the street as darkness shrouded the town. Most of the activity centered around the main street saloons and several men were loitering at the entrance of the one where he was headed. He crossed the muddy street and, with a pose of valid purpose, walked directly to his horse. This was a bold move and not a smart one at all, a great risk of recognition and capture.

The men loafing outside the Good Times Saloon paid little attention as Tom unwrapped the reins from the hitching rail. Ginger gave a snort of pleasured recognition and he caressed the mare's forelock as she nuzzled against him. He stepped into the stirrup and swung onto the saddle. Only one man glanced with slight interest as Tom pressed his right leg against the horse's side and with a slightest tug of the right rein turned her and rode away.

Tom resisted the impulse to spur the horse into a gallop, allowing an unhurried walk through the town center. At any moment, he expected an outcry of alarm, a hullabaloo of discovery. He stared ahead at the distant darkness beyond the outermost buildings of the town, a longed-for haven in which he could hide and disappear.

He gave a gentle tug on both reins and Ginger obediently stopped as two men crossed the street ahead of them. A large man with a badge on his shirt looked up and gave a nod of appreciation, then resumed an earnest conversation with his companion.

Tom let out a breath of relief and spurred the mare back to a slow walk.

Five minutes later, at the edge of the town, Tom leaned forward, whispered to the mare and, pressing his knees to her sides, nudged her into a trot.

Chapter Eighteen

Sheriff Morgan came awake at the first poundings on his front door. He rolled up to sit on the side of the bed, reached one hand for the revolver that hung from a belt on the bedpost and reached with the other to touch and calm his startled wife. "Lay quiet, Janey. Ain't likely a problem."

Nonetheless, his wife, a slender woman with a still-pretty face framed with tousled, graying hair, rose to a sitting position. "You never know, Will. Don't you be standing in the line of fire when you open that door."

The pounding on the door began again and a slurred voice shouted: "Morgan! Get your butt out here! Somebody stole my horse!"

Morgan sighed. "That damned Porter kid. Drunk again and raising hell." He rose to his feet and walked

137

out of the tiny bedroom, not at all concerned to be wearing only his cotton drawers. He wasn't concerned, either, at the bare belly that slightly protruded over the buttoned waistband. He was a big man and carried some extra weight with strength and remarkable agility for his middle age. He moved through the small living room of the four-room house and stood at one side of the door, his hand on the knob. "That you, Jed?"

"Damned right! Open the door! Somebody stole my horse!"

Morgan jerked the door open and, with the same hand, grabbed the front of Jed's suit coat and slammed him against the doorjamb. He took a quick glance to make sure Porter was alone. He looked down at Jed's waist and ran his hand over the suit coat. Satisfied that the young drunk carried no weapons, he re-gathered Jed's lapels and shook him violently. "What do you mean, this time of night, hammering on my door?"

"You're the sheriff, ain't you," Porter said in a weak voice. "Somebody took my horse."

"When?"

"I don't know. Left it outside while we was in the bar, gone when I come out."

"Sure you didn't misplace it?"

"No, sir. She were gone."

Morgan relaxed his grip and dropped his hand. "There's nothing I can do about it tonight. You find yourself somewhere to sleep it off. We'll talk about it in the morning."

"I want you to do something about it right now!" Porter demanded, regaining his conceit. "I want that horse back tonight!"

Morgan took the young man by the shoulders and turned him toward the street and gave him a small push to start him on his way. "We'll talk about it in the morning, son." He gauged the distance accurately and, despite feeling the top button of his underwear pop, swung his foot hard against Jed's buttocks. The young drunk pitched out onto the front walk and fell heavily on the gravel. With a groan, he rolled up on one forearm to stare at the near-naked man on the front stoop.

Pulling up his underwear, Morgan warned, "Come around again this time of night and I'll boot you all the way to that ranch you now call your own."

"I ain't forgetting this, Morgan."

"Good! Neither am I."

Morgan stepped back inside the house and closed the door behind him. He was surprised to see his wife in her nightgown standing in the doorframe of the bedroom, the weak shine of the quarter moon through the windows barely enough to show the smile on her face. Morgan responded with a huge grin. "Enjoyed seeing me doing my duty, did you?"

"I got a laugh out of seeing your drawers falling off while you were kicking him in the rear end." She joined him and looked through the window to watch Jed Porter stumbling back toward the main street. "Is he a problem?"

"Maybe. The wife of the fellow who is supposed to have killed his old man come to see me. She swears he wasn't the kind to do it."

"Isn't that what you'd expect her to say?"

Morgan cocked his head. "I 'spect. From all other folks' accounts, her man did the job, but—"

"But your gut feeling says different?"

Morgan shrugged. "Maybe I just never liked that bunch out there at that ranch. The old man came home from the war with some sorry stories told about him . . . and, well, you just saw the youngster."

"Best you sleep on it, Will. You only got about three hours before getting up time."

"Hell, I don't feel much like sleeping."

She smiled. "Well, come on anyway. We'll think of something to do."

Tom shifted his body to escape the discomfort of a pebble under his back. He had taken Ginger's saddle blanket for a makeshift bed on the hard ground. Whoever had taken his horse had removed his personal belongings from his saddlebags. Still, getting his mare back gave him a considerable lift of his spirits. She was tethered to a scrub brush several feet away, standing quiet, at peace in his presence. His affection for the animal was more than he had realized, a responsive companion on the trail. *A wanted man on foot, now a wanted man on horseback.*

He grimaced at his wry appraisal, recognizing that

although his mobility had changed his dilemma had not. The recovery of his horse could help him run faster from the law, but he would still be a fugitive, a hunted man. Finding Parrish had been his hope—finding him and, somehow, some way, making him confess to what really happened at the ranch. Perhaps the newspaperman would help, recalling their conversation about Parrish. Maybe the old man, Zeke, might know of something before he was struck down. Parrish might still be in Placerville or perhaps not. As he stared up at the starry sky, the entire hope began to fade, those possibilities seeming far-fetched.

He wriggled into a new position and closed his eyes, seeking sleep but finding his quandary instead.

Chapter Nineteen

Betty skipped the hotel's dining room breakfast, fearing to be seen by Langdon Sherwood. Ever since she had caught sight of the group led by the diminutive lawyer, she had kept to her room to avoid an encounter. Now, as she swiftly descended the steps, she made sure that none of them loitered in the lobby. A glance at a wall clock showed the morning hour past nine as she hurried out the front door.

The morning was bright and clear and the sun had dried the mucky streets. Nonetheless, she lifted the hem of her long skirt as she picked her path to the opposite boardwalk and turned toward the jail. To her surprise, Sheriff Morgan was striding toward her, his head down and apparently deep in thought.

"Good morning, Sheriff," she said as he came abreast of her.

Morgan looked up, obviously exasperated by the sight of her. "Mrs. Patterson," he acknowledged. "You haven't gone home."

"No . . . and I want to talk with you."

"Not now. I haven't got the time." He touched the brim of his hat and walked past her.

Betty whirled and hastened to walk side by side with him on the boardwalk. "This is important, Sheriff."

"Ma'am"—Morgan sighed his annoyance—"if you want to wait at my office, I'll be back after I take care of another matter."

"What's so important?"

"Horse been stolen." The lawman did not break his stride.

"There's someone here in town you should question."

"Ma'am, I'm trying to be polite, but you're trying my patience."

"And you, mine."

Morgan stopped walking and turned to face her. "If it's so damned important then tell me about it as we go. Kill two birds with one stone."

They resumed along the boardwalk.

"Tom and I went to see a lawyer in Sacramento about the man I told you about yesterday."

"Go on."

"He's here . . . the lawyer I mean . . . at the hotel," she told him. "And there's a man with him that looks just like the one who tried to hire Tom."

"This man . . . what did he look like?"

"Big man like Tom said. Dark hair, beard and had that scar. Dresses fancy. Hotel clerk said he was registered as Carl Parrish."

Morgan pursed his lips and his brow furrowed. "Parrish, hmm. Sounds sorta familiar." He came to a stop at the open doors of a small saloon. "If you don't mind waiting out here, I'll just be a few minutes."

"You looking for a stolen horse in there?"

Morgan gave her a pained look and walked through the doors.

Betty hesitated and then followed.

Morgan looked back with a greater aggravation. "Mrs. Patterson, this is no place for a lady."

"Don't worry about me, Sheriff. Nothing here I ain't seen in my life."

The barroom was gray and grimy, ugly in the midmorning light. Only three people were in the Good Times Saloon, a bartender and an early drinker on either side of the scuffed, battered pine wood bar, and a young woman eating breakfast at a table. Ancient flower-patterned wallpaper was peeling loose in places at the ceiling, unwashed glasses had been left on several tables and the floor was still littered with food droppings and cigar butts from the night before.

With a disapproving glance at Betty and a shrug,

Morgan walked to the bar and signaled for the bartender's attention.

"Help you, Sheriff?"

"Heard tell young Porter was hollering about losing his horse while he was here last night."

The bartender gave a nod. "Bitched about it soon as he found out. We was wanting to close up but he wouldn't have it. Kept us here to all hours wanting to know if I'd seen anything. Drunk as a dad-burned skunk, he was."

"He's still sobering up somewhere, I guess. Did you see anybody?"

"Nope." The bartender looked past the lawman at Betty. "Maybe that lady shouldn't be in here."

"Told her so but she's not one to listen."

"I'll try to watch my swearing."

Morgan turned his attention to the young woman at the table. "What about you, Dorie? See anybody take his horse?"

The young woman looked up and shook her head emphatically. "Didn't know anything 'til Jed came hollering back in here about it. Making a big noise about it but it wasn't even his nag. He'd been bragging to his pals that he took him off that fellow that shot his old man."

Betty charged across the room to the table. "She's talking about Ginger!"

"Who's Ginger?" a bewildered Morgan asked as he hurried to join her.

"Tom's mare! What was this Jed fellow doing riding Tom's horse?"

Unsettled by the rush to her table, the girl pushed back in her chair and darted quick glances between the lawman and the demanding woman. "What's going on here?"

"What else did he say?" Betty persisted.

"Something about his own horse being shot out from under him and that's why he was taking this 'un."

"First I've heard about any horse shooting," the sheriff exclaimed. "When did this happen?"

"I don't know," the girl responded. "Just that somebody shot his danged horse."

"Somebody?" Morgan questioned. "That's what he said? *Somebody* shot his horse?"

The girl lifted her shoulders. "That's all I heard."

"He didn't say *Patterson* shot the horse?" the sheriff asked.

Showing exasperation, Dorie shook her head. "No, just that somebody shot his horse out from under him while they was riding along."

"Who's they?" Morgan kept at her. "Riding along where?"

The girl looked puzzled. "I just heard bits and pieces of their dumb talk. I don't listen to all what drunks say."

"His pals? That'd be Dave Moody and Bobby Shultz?"

Dorie nodded.

"What are you thinking, Sheriff?" Betty asked.

"I'm thinking I want to talk to those two buddies of Jed's," the lawman answered. "Maybe we can get a lot more of what they were saying last night."

"You coming around to what I've been saying, Sheriff?" Betty asked.

"Too early for that," Morgan responded. "You come back to my office and we'll see."

"Hope I've been some help," Dorie volunteered.

Betty gave her a wide smile. "More than you know, dear."

"Something else," Morgan said as he took Betty gently by the arm and steered her toward the door. "I think maybe we both got an idea about who took that horse."

Langdon Sherwood waved good-bye to his business associates as the stage to Virginia City pulled away from the hotel. They'd grumbled about the hard, dusty ride ahead and grouched about having to come to Placerville for this conference. He had affected a conciliatory attitude, explaining a halfway meeting site important to his busy schedule.

A sunlight flash from a lawman's badge across the street caught his attention but his interest immediately focused upon the woman walking with him. He recognized her instantly, the wife of Tom Patterson. He observed they were in earnest conversation as they walked together, the lawman listening and attentive.

He walked back into the hotel, entered the lobby and found Parrish coming down the steps. He motioned the big man to an area out of the hearing of the desk clerk and spoke softly. "Carl, I just saw the Patterson woman on the street walking with the local law."

Parrish gave him a blank stare. "What's she doing here?"

The lawyer shook his head. "I don't like it. I hope she didn't see either of us."

"She don't know me."

"Well, she knows me and I don't like her nosing around." He pulled a watch from his vest pocket, opened it and noted the time. "I'm catching the train back to Sacramento and I want you back to your hideout right now."

"Now?"

The lawyer nodded. "This thing is getting out of hand. Patterson should've been laying dead, gun in hand, across from Porter and there'd been no questions asked. Maybe he's dead up there in the mountains or, more likely, he's alive. You've botched what should've been a simple job and it's getting worse."

"He's on the run, what can he do?" Parrish argued angrily. "I've always done good for you. Everything's going to be fine, you wait and see."

"It'd better be." Sherwood snapped the watch closed and replaced it in his vest pocket. "I don't want him caught and I don't want him talking. I don't like seeing his wife being cozy with that lawman and I sure don't like what I've been hearing about that fool boy. I heard he was drinking pretty hard after the funeral."

"I'll talk to him," Parrish promised. "Before I leave."

"I'd have him killed if we didn't need him."

"Maybe after it's over," Parrish said with a smirk.

"Before he gets drunk in 'Frisco and starts telling things."

"Something we should probably consider. We're close, Carl. Don't let anything else go wrong. You've got to find Patterson and end it once and for all."

"I won't fail you, Mr. Sherwood."

"Fail me and we all fail."

Chapter Twenty

Jed Porter's sleep ended abruptly as a big hand shook him violently. "Wha–a–a?" he moaned, trying to fan away the alcoholic daze that blurred his vision and his speech. "That you, Parrish?"

The big man reached down and gripped Jed's bare shoulders and hauled him out of the bed. "Get up!" Parrish commanded.

"Okay, okay. Let me alone . . . I'm up." Jed looked around for his trousers. "Where's the girl?"

"Downstairs if she knows what's good for her."

"Whatcha so mad about?"

"You getting drunk and, for all we know, shooting your mouth off. You get yourself dressed and back to the ranch."

"I ain't said nothing," Jed declared.

"Hope not. For your sake."

"Somebody stole my horse," the young man complained. "That's why I had to stay in town."

"I heard you was riding Patterson's horse."

"Well, hell, you shot mine."

"Let me tell you something, boy. You get on home and stay outta this town or any other place 'til this whole shenanigan is over and done. You, me, all of us, we're going to get rich unless you play the fool and ruin everything. You sell the ranch to us and your part is over."

Jed found his shirt and trousers under the bed and began to dress. "You coming with me?"

Parrish shook his head. "You got your man, Sam, to stay out there with you. Maybe, later, I'll send a couple of others along."

"Why?"

"Just on the chance Patterson might come out of the backcountry to your place."

"Why would he do that?"

"Because he goes left when he ought to go right," Parrish grumbled. " 'Cause he jumps when he ought to squat! Luckiest man I ever seen. Fifteen, sixteen bullets with his name on each and every one and he ducks them all."

"That luck can't last," Jed said as he buttoned his pants.

"Sherwood may think he's the top rung on the ladder, but he was the one with the bright idea of bringing Patterson in on this thing. Had my way, I'd have shot your pa and we'd have got on with it." Parrish opened the door of the room and gave a sweeping gesture. "Get outta here and on home."

Impatient, Sherwood shifted the valise from his right hand to his left and took the pocket watch from his vest. He was standing with seven other people on the platform, waiting for the conductor to appear and give the signal to board. He looked at the locomotive emitting negligible puffs of steam as the fireman and engineer took their time to build the necessary pressure.

The short train carried only one passenger coach and four boxcars. At the end of the line from Sacramento, the station building showed activity only when the train arrived in the evening and, again, when it made the return trip the following morning. Sidings showed little evidence of frequent use, rust on the rails and weeds growing profusely between the ties. Two dilapidated boxcars were the only rolling stock parked on a spur.

With the dwindling of commercial traffic on the wagon road, the passenger ridership and freight hauling on the train had diminished to a near unprofitable status. Management of the Central Pacific considered this rail extension more a liability than an asset and management's plan to abandon it was an oft-repeated option.

"Mr. Sherwood?"

The attorney turned, startled at the sight of the tall lawman.

"Mr. Sherwood, I'm Sheriff Morgan. I know your train is going to leave in a few minutes, but could I take a bit of your time?"

"What's this about, Sheriff?" Sherwood let his irritation show.

"A few questions."

"I haven't the time—"

"We'll take the time. I tried to catch you at the hotel. Desk clerk told me you was taking the train."

"Which is about to leave," Sherwood said, seeing the conductor step from the coach and assist passengers aboard. "Now, if you'll excuse me—"

"Desk clerk told me you've been having a meeting with several folks."

"That's none of your business, Sheriff."

"Wayne . . . that's the desk clerk . . . he was telling me about this big fellow. Dark hair and beard over a scar, a bit of a swell he was saying. Said he was registered as Carl Parrish. Wayne said he was with you most of the time."

"What of it?"

"Fellow fits a description. Story is that he might be involved in something not so good."

"Such as?"

"Well, like maybe trying to hire a killing."

"That's claptrap, Sheriff!" Sherwood exploded. "Wherever you got that notion, it's nonsense!"

"Likely so. Still, I'd like to know what dealings you have with the man."

"None of your business, sir."

"Not a polite answer, Mr. Sherwood."

The lawyer sighed his exasperation. "Look here! You're going to make me miss my train."

"Plenty of time. They're still loading that third boxcar."

"I barely know this man, Parrish. He's done some work for me from time to time."

"What sort of work?"

"Really now, Sheriff—"

"Explain it to me now or we'll go back to my office."

For a full minute, the undersized man didn't speak, glaring up at the sheriff's stern face.

"What sort of work?" Morgan asked again.

"Very well," Sherwood began hesitantly. "On a very few occasions, the railroad has hired Mr. Parrish to assist in finding and acquiring land properties."

"Involved in that Mussel Slough affair last spring?"

"I wouldn't know about that. As I said, I barely know the man and I know nothing about any of his activities. He is currently providing me with some information but that is the extent of it. Nothing unlawful, I assure you."

"You do your lawyering for Central Pacific?"

Sherwood shook his head. "Not anymore. I'm in business for myself."

"And what might that business be?"

"I represent investors in various projects, Sheriff,"

Sherwood said coolly. "Now, unless you have some sort of a reason to continue this nonsense, the conversation is over."

"One more question," Morgan said easily. "Where can I find Parrish?"

Three short blasts from the locomotive whistle gave the signal that the train was ready to roll.

"My train, officer. I must go."

"Know where Parrish might be?"

The lawyer shook his head. "I have no idea at all. May I leave?"

"Have a good trip, Mr. Sherwood. I may want to contact you some time in the future."

"By all means, Sheriff," Sherwood said as he began to trot toward the train. "Anything I can ever do to help the law."

Betty walked from behind the station corner to join the sheriff as the lawyer stepped up into the coach and disappeared from view. "Did you learn anything, Sheriff?"

"I think so," Morgan said with a nod. "This don't take the hassle off your man, but it does raise some mighty interesting possibilities."

"You believe me?"

"Beginning to, ma' am. It' s not my job to go against things as they appear to be, but you can't rule out what my wife calls my 'gut feelings.' "

Betty smiled. "Tom's like that. He's got a sense about

different people, who they are or, sometimes, who they pretend to be." She paused. "You and he are a lot alike, Sheriff Morgan."

"I guess I could take that as a compliment," he responded with a rueful grin. "Now—"

"I think it's time for me to head home," Betty interrupted. "Nothing more here I can do. I'll leave tomorrow morning."

The sheriff's smile creased seldom-seen wrinkles in the weathered face. "We are beginning to understand each other."

Tom stood at the crest of a hill overlooking the road west of Placerville. He had heard the far-off train whistle over an hour ago and, in the distance, seen the plume of black smoke rising and trailing over the intervening small hills as it passed on the way to Sacramento.

Parrish could be on that train.

He had wrestled with his problems all through his restless night. The desire to stay free and uncaged was almost irresistible. In his younger days, it would have been all right, living on the dodge, staying in the fringes and shadows of this community or that, never in one place or another for any period of days. But he was different now, older, becoming settled in a comfortable way. Now, he was a man who had, over time, come to respect the law and enforced it—even to trust it.

He stepped into a stirrup, swung into the saddle and, with a slight forward lean, urged Ginger into a walk.

The morning traffic on the road below was moderately active, single and companioned riders on horseback, wagons, buckboards and buggies moving in both directions. Tom turned his mare toward Placerville and rode in between two freight-hauling Conestoga wagons.

Tom had differing views concerning Western lawmen. In those times he had worn a badge, he had worked with a number of them. All were tough men, physically strong and purposeful in their actions. Quite a few were nearly as bad as the desperados they pursued, caught, shot or hung. Some were as dishonest as the crooks they jailed and a sizable group received illicit pay from saloon and brothel owners. Still, a substantial number of fair and just men were in the profession. Tom hoped one of the latter would represent the law in Placerville.

Surrendering in the middle of the day with the town at its peak of activity was a deliberate decision. Tom wanted dozens and dozens of witnesses to attest to his willing submission to the law. He considered it far better to give himself up rather than to be captured as a fugitive.

At the edge of town, he rode Ginger slightly behind and with her head nosed between two other horseback riders. From a casual observer's point of view, it might appear that he was a companion to the others. They moved along the main street into Placerville's heart of commerce. He spied the jail only two blocks away and he continued his journey toward that destination.

At a crosswalk, he reined up as pedestrians moved across the street in front of him. He was about to spur his mare forward when, on the corner, he saw the same lawman he had seen the night before.

Betty is with him!

The two were in earnest conversation as they stepped into the street and Tom was not at all sure Betty had spotted him. As they passed before him, his wife's eyes never glanced in his direction, her animated discussion captivating her outsized companion. Only as they reached the other side of the street did Tom see Betty's hand at her side, her fingers waving him on, a warning.

Tom tugged the reins and turned Ginger into a side street where he dismounted and tied her to a hitching rail in front of a feed store. In a casual manner, he sauntered to the corner and assumed a loitering pose, his eyes following his wife and the lawman. From a distance, he watched the pantomime as the big man was bidding Betty a courteous farewell. Betty gave an appreciative nod and turned to walk away. The lawman watched her for a moment and then he, too, turned and walked toward the jail.

Tom watched his wife as she crossed to his side of the street and walked to the hotel. Although two blocks away, he saw her pause, glance in his direction, then enter the building. He returned to Ginger, gave her a pat of reassurance on the nose and walked down a back alley to approach the hotel.

There were two back doors to the hotel, one from the kitchen, the other a rear access to the main corridor and a back stairway. Making sure he was unseen, he entered the second door and hurried up the steps to the upper floor.

"Tom!" came an urgent soft-spoken call.

Betty was waiting at the open door of her room as he ran to gather her in his arms. His wife hugged him fiercely, the side of her face on his chest. "I saw you but couldn't believe it!"

"What are you doing here?" he asked as they moved into the room and closed the door. "When did you come?"

"You're in trouble . . . where else would I be?" Betty leaned away to look up at his face. "Lord, Tom, I was afraid."

"Me, too," he said with a wry grin. He kissed her and kept her in his embrace for a long time.

"Where were you going?" Betty asked as she drew back to regard him.

"To give myself up. I couldn't stay on the run. Sooner or later, they'd get me." He shook his head. "Bett, I didn't kill anybody."

"I knew. All the time, I really knew."

"What are they saying here in town?"

"That you killed both of them. Shot Porter and beat the other fellow to death." She shuddered. "When I heard that, I knew it wasn't you."

"Beat the other fellow? The kid?"

Betty showed her confusion. "What kid?"

"The Porter kid. Young fellow."

"You mean Jed Porter?"

Tom nodded.

"He ain't dead. He's in town making all kinds of accusations."

"Alive?" Tom questioned, the news overwhelming him. "Well, who in the hell got beat to death?"

"The old man. They called him Zeke."

Tom rolled his eyes. "I found that old codger laying on the ground outside the bunkhouse. Somebody had rapped him pretty good on the head, but he was okay, still alive." He took Betty's shoulders in his hands. "I saw that Jed Porter laying on the ground in his own blood and his pa standing and grieving over him and saying I done it. That's why he was shooting at me."

"All I can tell you is Jed Porter ain't dead." This don't make no sense."

"Say that for sure." He dropped his hands and sat down in a chair. "Let me tell you what happened."

Betty listened attentively as Tom recounted the shooting encounter at the ranch and, briefly, his subsequent escape.

"That Jed kid must've been play acting like he was dead," she ventured.

"He did a hell of a good job of it. Had his pa plumb convinced."

"You actually climbed a danged cliff?" She chortled. "I'd like to have seen that."

"You been where I was up there, you'd have had yourself a heart attack."

Betty's face sobered. "You *were* going to give yourself up?"

Tom nodded. "Take my chances. Stay on the run, I'm likely to be shot dead on sight."

"The sheriff's name is Morgan. He's a good man and fair."

"Maybe."

"That's what I've been doing, Tom. Talking with Sheriff Morgan, telling him that you wasn't the sort to do what they said. I think he does believe me."

"I got no proof, Bett. Everybody's word against mine."

"That ain't quite so. I spotted the little lawyer, Sherwood, in town and, I think that Parrish man was with him."

Tom gave a low whistle. "They both still there?"

She shook her head. "Sherwood left on the train and I don't know about Parrish. I didn't see him at the station so maybe he's still in town."

"Even if I was to find him, there ain't no way I'm gonna make him tell the truth."

Betty crossed her arms and paced the room. "Way I see it, it ain't all that bad. We got a sheriff who's beginning to come around. We got this Parrish who's got a bad name in these parts." She stopped and faced her husband. "And there was a bunch of high-falutin' gents here in the hotel with Sherwood and Parrish. Maybe somebody ought to find out what that was all about."

"I got an idea about that."

She gave him a quizzical look.

"When I was up on top of that canyon, it seemed to me that it wouldn't take too much to tunnel through and build a rail line up into the Tahoe area. Just a guess, but with that lawyer being in the railroad business, maybe Captain Portee . . . that is, rancher Porter, was the holdup. His kid told me he wouldn't sell his place and was plumb loco not to. Maybe this whole thing from the start was just to get rid of him."

"And what about those gents meeting with that shyster?"

"Betcha they was in on putting up money for the shebang."

"How'd you come by that idea?"

"Was talking to that newspaper editor, him telling about how this town and some others got bypassed by the rails going north of here."

Betty made a face. "You should read what that newspaper fellow said about you! Calling you a killer and saying you was hunting for Porter—"

"What? Are we talking about the same newspaper guy?"

She nodded. "Said terrible things."

Tom leaned forward with his chin resting on his folded hands, his elbows on his knees. "That's a bother," he said softly. "Could be he's in on it too."

"What do you mean?"

"In them articles, he say anything about me looking for Parrish?"

She shook her head.

"Well, that's who I told him I was after. Fellow seemed downright accommodating. Come to remembering, he's the one who steered me up toward Nevada and let on I'd find Parrish there."

"And young Jed Porter just happened to be riding on that very same road that day!" Betty exclaimed.

"You got yourself a dumb husband," Tom said and leaned back in the chair. "Set me up like a damned fool." He cocked his head and gave her a wry smile. "You *was* the lady who told me to let it go. I shoulda listened."

"If you had, these crooks would've gotten away with everything."

"They may yet." He rose to his feet and walked to the window to look out. "Think I should give up to your Sheriff Morgan?"

Betty walked close to encircle his waist with her arm. "Maybe not just yet, darling. Not much you can do inside a jail cell."

Tom nodded. "Was that young Jed who was riding my Ginger?"

She nodded. "Made a big fuss about you taking her back." She laughed. "The sheriff guessed it might be you."

"Well, then, I guess he knows I'm hereabouts." Tom

stepped away from the window taking Betty with him. "I got an idea about later this evening . . . best I wait 'til then right here in this room."

"Long as you're mighty quiet," she cautioned.

He gave her a questioning look.

She gave him a mischievous smile in return. "Charge me extra if I have a man in my room."

Chapter Twenty-one

Despite the still-bright daylight of the evening, Tom came out of the rear of the hotel, a gamble that he could move unrecognized toward his destination. He walked to the main street and fell in behind two tradesmen as they ambled along the boardwalk, his head lowered and Ike's battered hat tilted slightly forward. He touched the brim as if giving a friendly salute to both men and women as they approached him, his raised hand concealing a full view of his face.

Across the street from the *Placerville Weekly Press,* he stopped in the deep shade of a building's overhang. He loitered there in the company of two blowsy drunks who were trying to sober up before starting their nighttime binges. Within fifteen minutes, he saw the elderly lady emerge from the front door of the newspaper office and saw movement inside. It appeared the editor was working into the seven o'clock hour.

Tom surveyed the slackening pace of pedestrian and horse and carriage traffic and quickly crossed to the other side of the street. He strode to the front door of the newspaper office and, surprised to find it unlocked, swung it open and stepped inside.

John Driscoll looked up, his annoyed expression changing immediately to one of shock and alarm. "My . . . my God," he stammered.

Tom drew his Colt and used it to point to the pressroom. "We need to talk. Anybody back there?"

Speechless, Driscoll shook his head.

"Good, let's go."

Driscoll looked past Tom for help from the street. Seeing no one, he walked meekly into the pressroom, finally finding his voice. "What are you going to do?"

"Depends on you. You and your friends have put me in one hell of a spot. I'm likely to be a dead man because of your conniving. It surely seems fair you have the same prospects."

"I didn't do anything," Driscoll whimpered.

"You put me on the trail of Parrish and, I 'spect, sent young Porter to ride along with me."

"I didn't have anything to do with—"

Tom pulled the hammer back on the revolver. "Want to keep arguing?"

The editor slumped, eyes fastened on the gun's barrel.

"Did Parrish tell you what to say?"

The editor hesitated and then nodded.

"Your paper comes out when?"

Driscoll gave him an odd look. "Day after tomorrow."

Tom walked to the printing press, looked down at the type forms and shook his head. "Nope, it comes out tomorrow. Kind of a special, you might say."

"A special what?"

"What your headline's gonna say is, 'TOM PATTER-SON'S SIDE OF THE STORY.'"

"I can't do that."

Tom leveled his revolver. "Sit down and take pen in hand. We're going to write us the true piece of the goings-on at the Porter ranch."

"You a married man?" Tom asked the editor shortly before dawn.

Driscoll shook his head as he finished locking the type into the forms. "Used to be, but she's gone."

"Passed away?"

Driscoll shook his head again. "Took off for back East with a corset drummer and my young one a few years ago."

"Well, anyone that'd be concerned you didn't come home last night?"

"No," Driscoll muttered and gestured to the press. "I'm a dead man if I print this."

"You are for sure if you don't."

"You've made wild accusations and defamed me—"

"Nothing more than you deserve."

"It's your word against upright citizens of this county and who'll believe it?"

"Well, it'll sure give folks something to think about. Maybe those upright citizens might have to do some better explaining." Tom rose from the chair and walked to the doorway to the front office. "What time does your help come in?"

"Mrs. Palmquist comes in at nine. My devil comes in late this afternoon."

"Devil?"

"Printer's devil. My helper."

"Reckon you'll have to be your own devil this morning." Tom chuckled. "There's a handle that surely fits you." He walked back to join Driscoll at the press. "When the lady comes in, you tell her you're giving her the morning off."

"I've never done that. She'll wonder why."

"Tell her you're softhearted and turning over a new leaf."

"She won't believe that either."

"I don't care what you tell her, but make sure she stays away while we're printing."

"Once she sees the paper—"

"Won't make no difference once it's out in the street."

"You're going against some powerful men in this

state," Driscoll said. "They'll take severe measures against you."

Tom laughed. "You mean they ain't already? Seems like to me them tables have turned in my direction for a change. Some time this afternoon, we'll see."

Chapter Twenty-two

Betty trod the boardwalk with a lively step, the *Placerville Weekly Press Special Edition* in her hand. An hour earlier, young boys had crisscrossed the main avenue with their burdens of newspapers. They had delivered copies to people in stores they entered and handed the paper to each pedestrian or idler they met on the street.

"Lookee here," she heard one sidewalk reader say to another as she passed. "It says that Porter kid helped kill his old man."

"Knowing that young rowdy, I wouldn't put it past him," responded the second man.

Betty turned at the entrance of the sheriff's office, opened the door and walked in. The three deputies were seated in chairs, each with a newspaper opened. At the back of the office area, Sheriff Morgan was hunched over the same paper, engrossed in his reading. Reacting slowly from his study, he looked up and a scowl appeared. "Mrs. Patterson," he said loudly. "What in tarnation have I done to deserve you people?"

Betty let herself through the railing gate and walked directly to Morgan's desk, flourishing her copy of the paper. "You've read Tom's piece?"

"Reading it," the lawman countered. "He couldn't have come direct to me?"

"No offense, Sheriff," she half-apologized. "He was surely planning to, but he thought this might be a safer way. He don't know you, you see."

"I take it you've seen him?"

She nodded. "Never you mind about that. Do you believe what he's said there?"

"Where is he?"

"You believe what he says?"

"I'm thinking on it. Now, one more time . . . where is he?

"Over at the newspaper office, waiting for you."

"Damnation. Sorry, ma'am, shouldn't swear in front of you although I think I got cause."

"Shall we go?"

"We?" The sheriff rose to his feet and looked past her. "Nick, you and Mitch come along, we're going to join Mr. Patterson at the press office." He looked directly at Betty. "You stay here."

"Whatever you say. Where may I sit?"

"Try one of the cells," the sheriff grumbled. "No, just sit anywhere. Your husband armed?"

"He's laid his guns aside. He ain't looking for a shooting match."

"Better not," Morgan grumped as he headed for the door. "Gus, keep an eye on her." He waved his hand to the remaining pair. "Come on, boys."

Betty chose the chair of one of the men who followed the sheriff out of the building and turned to the one young man who'd been left behind. "Don't you worry, Gus. I'll just sit here and be real good."

Sheriff Morgan led his deputies in a striding march down the boardwalk toward the *Placerville Weekly Press* building, drawing his own six-shooter and signaling his men to do the same. They approached the entry door of the newspaper office with caution, Morgan peering in the front window. Tom, unarmed and in plain sight, motioned for the sheriff to enter.

"Sheriff Morgan," Tom said as the trio walked into the office. "Heard some good things about you."

"Tom Patterson, I'm about as wound up as I can be and I ain't in no mood for your howdy-do palaver."

"The newspaper account?" Tom questioned and nodded. "Only way I could think to get my story told . . . just in case those good things I heard about you might not be the fact."

"I told your wife I was fair," the sheriff blustered.

"I'm hoping that's true."

The lawman turned to the newspaper editor sitting dejectedly at his desk. "You all right, John?"

"He had me under duress, Sheriff!" Driscoll whined. "Had his gun on me."

"What's said in the paper? Is it true?" Morgan asked.

"No, sir. Not a word of it," Driscoll declared.

"He's lying," Tom said easily. "Not about being under my gun, that's true, but what was said in that piece, don't that sorta fall in place for you?"

"Maybe," Morgan admitted.

"Arrest him, Sheriff," Driscoll said. "I'll proffer charges."

"We ain't quite to that point yet, John," Morgan said. "We'll talk later." He turned his attention to Tom. "You've been on the run, a fugitive."

"You read the piece, six or more gunhands shooting at me and me climbing a damned mountain in the dark. What would you expect me to do?"

"To give yourself up to the law."

"And how was I to know who was the law and who wasn't? Soon as I got clear, I come into town, cornered this greedy fellow here and made him print my story. I'm giving myself up to you right now peaceable. I ain't shot or hurt anybody and that includes those two at the ranch."

"He had a grudge against Ed Porter," the editor said in a quavering voice. "They were war enemies!"

"Captain Edward Portee was court-marshaled and disgraced," Tom said. "What he done in the war likely deserved killing, but I'd have left that to heaven."

"Sheriff, who's going to pay for printing that nonsense? I demand—"

"Shut up, John," Morgan cut in. "Time comes, I want to have a long talk with you. You got some explaining to do." He waved his revolver at the door. "Walk ahead of me, Patterson. Your missus is waiting down at the jail." He turned to his deputies. "Nick, pick up his Colt and that little gun there."

With Driscoll uttering words of protest and dismay, Tom walked out the door, the sheriff and his deputies forming a pocket around him.

"You still thinking I'm the killer?" Tom asked as they walked.

"I'm thinking on it," Morgan replied. "Save talk 'til we get to the jail." He turned to his men. "Holster your pistols, boys. No use in making a show out of this."

Even so, people gawked as the lawmen escorted Tom down the street.

A man on horseback shouted, "Is that Patterson, Sheriff?"

"Mind your own business, Archie! We'll mind ours!"

Nonetheless, a considerable number of people abandoned their own concerns and trailed after the four men. At the entrance to the jail, Sheriff Morgan waved Tom and his deputies inside while he turned to confront the gathering of the curious. "Folks, go on about your own business. There ain't nothing that I can tell you now. We're investigating—"

"Is that Patterson a prisoner?" one man interrupted.

"I ain't prepared to say. Mr. Patterson did come in on his own and he's here to answer some questions. You all go on. When we got something to say, we'll let everybody know."

"That story in the paper true, Will?" came another voice.

Morgan turned away without answering and entered the jail.

"Am I a prisoner, Sheriff?" Tom was standing just inside the door in the entry area, a deputy on either side. Betty was standing several feet away on the other side of the railing.

"For the time being, yes, sir," Morgan acknowledged. "Mitch, you and Gus put him in a cell back there, lock him up and come on back."

"Put the lady in there too?" Deputy Gus asked.

Morgan rolled his eyes. "No, but you might look in her handbag, see if she's carrying a hacksaw." He fixed Betty with a meaningful stare. "You might as well go on back to the hotel and stay put for a change."

"For how long?"

"Until I have a chance to do some sheriffing," he grumped. "I'm holding your husband, let's say as a material witness. I'm going out to the Porter ranch and bringing Jed and his hired hand in here for questioning. That okay with the two of you?"

"Mighty fine, Sheriff," Betty responded and walked

through the railing gate and hesitated as she opened the door. "And thank you." She glanced at her husband, gave him a nod and stepped out onto the boardwalk.

. Deputy Gus took three steps toward the door before he turned to the sheriff. "Was you serious, Will?"

"About what"

"Checking for a hacksaw?"

Chapter Twenty-three

Sheriff Morgan reined in his horse some distance from the Porter ranch and signaled his deputies, Nick and Mitch, to do so as well. "We'll come in spread out, not a bunched-up target," he instructed. "There may not be any trouble, but that boy, Jed, no telling what he might do."

"You think Patterson's got it right?" Nick asked.

"That's what we're here to find out. You fellows stay back while I ride in a little and give the house a shout."

"Not too near, Will," Mitch cautioned.

"I'll do what I have to do," the sheriff responded. He spurred his horse and rode to the perimeter of the ranch structures. "Jed Porter!" he shouted. "This is Sheriff Morgan! Me and my deputies are coming in! We need to have a little talk with you and Sam! Come on out into the yard!"

There was no answer; only the soft sound of wind whispering occasionally through the outbuildings and corral rails. Morgan listened intently, straining to hear any sounds from inside the house, any crunch of a footstep on the crusty soil of the backyard. He sat very still for a long time, his eyes sweeping the set of buildings, peering into the dark corners. Finally, he raised his hand and waved his deputies forward and each, keeping a distance from one another, rode into the center of the compound.

"Nobody here, Will," Nick ventured as he rode close.

"Get off and keep your horse between you and the house," Morgan commanded as he dismounted. "Mitch, check the barn!"

Guns drawn and hunched behind their horses, Morgan and Nick moved toward the ranch house. Mitch slipped from his saddle and led his horse to the barn. With the reins still in one hand and a revolver in the other, he flattened his back against the front planks as he edged toward the open door. Morgan and Nick rushed from the shielding horses to the portico of the house, one on either side of the front door.

"Jed!" Morgan yelled. "Come on out, son! Don't do anything foolish!"

"Will!"

Morgan and Nick whirled at Mitch's shout.

"We got someone here!"

Out of the interior gloom of the barn, a dark figure emerged into the sunlight, a slender, unkempt young man with his hands held high. "It's me, Sheriff! It' s me . . . Sam Jarett."

"Anybody in there with you, Sam?" Morgan questioned.

"No, sir, just me," Sam's voice quavered.

"Where's Jed?"

"Gone, Sheriff. Lit out 'while back."

"He's not in the house?"

"No, he's gone. On his pa's horse and gone."

Morgan waved his revolver to the ranch house door. "Check it out anyway, Nick. And be careful."

The young deputy nodded and eased into the house.

Morgan lowered his revolver as he stepped away from the house and walked out to join Mitch and the hired hand. "Take his gun, Mitch," he ordered. "Was you hiding from us?"

"No, Sheriff," the man answered, his hands still held high as Mitch took his side arm. "From Mr. Jed."

"From Jed? What for?"

"I didn't want him to do me like he did Zeke."

The sheriff regarded the cowering ranch hand, recalling the man was six inches shy of a feeble mind. "You can put your hands down, Sam."

Sam kept his hands over his head. "Don't shoot me, Mr. Sheriff." Stepping close behind him, Mitch gently pulled the frightened man's hands to his sides.

"Did Jed kill Zeke?" Morgan asked.

Sam nodded. "I didn't see it, but he must've."

"It wasn't Patterson?"

"Who?"

"The man who was here that night. The night Zeke and Mr. Porter got killed?"

"They said I should say so," Sam told them. "He was still laying there breathing after that man went up the mountain."

Nick came out of the ranch house shaking his head. "Not in there, Will. He must've lit out like Sam says."

"Why would you think Jed would do something to you?" Morgan asked.

The ranch hand lowered his eyes to the ground. "He was looking for me 'fore he left, shouting like you all for me to come out." Sam shook his head at the memory. "He was mad, really mad when he couldn't find me. He got on his horse and shouting he'd kill me if I said something 'bout things."

"It's all right, Sam," Morgan said in a soft, consoling voice. "He ain't going to hurt you. We'll make sure."

"You going to put me in jail, Mr. Sheriff?"

"Maybe so, maybe not, Sam. You didn't do any of the killing, did you?"

"Shot a few times at the man on the mountain," Sam admitted. "I ain't a very good shot."

"Don't worry about it, Sam. Mitch, help him saddle up his horse and let's get him on back to town."

The deputy nodded and took Sam by the arm and led him back into the barn.

Nick returned his revolver to his holster and stepped close to his boss. "Looks like Patterson's in the clear."

Morgan nodded. "Suppose so."

"In a way, that's too bad."

Morgan looked at his deputy in surprise.

"Shoot, with him out of the way," Nick said, a wide grin sliding across his face, "that pretty wife of his might just have taken a shine to me."

Morgan eyed his plain-faced deputy and chuckled. "You got a wicked mind, Nicky, and I surely do admire you for it, but, hell, boy, she's far too much of a woman for the likes of you."

Mitch came out of the barn with Sam and his horse and wondered what the two men were laughing about.

With the ranch hand, Sam, in a cell and the newspaper editor in another, the sheriff ushered Tom and Betty into the windowless room. "Best place to talk, I got," Morgan apologized. "Sit and we'll get things straight."

Tom held a chair for Betty, then seated himself while the lawman remained standing.

"From what poor old Sam has said and with Driscoll spilling his part of it, looks like I got no reason to hold you," Morgan said. "We'll be posting warrants for Carl Parrish and Jedidiah Porter."

"What about the one out for me?" Tom asked.

"Telegrams gone out to most places," the sheriff assured him. "Best you carry an official letter from me. Pick it up before you leave."

"Hope they believe it."

"What about that pip-squeak lawyer?" Betty asked. "And the men with him at the hotel?"

"We wired the Sacramento police," Morgan said. "They'll be paying the little scoundrel a visit. The others? Likely just greedy men who bought into Sherwood's get rich scheme, but I don't suppose they were involved in the killings. We'll see what they have to say."

"Then, we're free to head home?" Tom asked.

Morgan nodded and rose to his feet, the Patterson couple rising with him. The lawman extended his hand to Tom. "It pleases me to say you are." He smiled at Betty. "You're a lucky man with this lady. She's got a belief in you that made a believer out of me."

"She's a dandy," Tom agreed.

"Go on with you two," Betty murmured, her smiling face taking on a high radiance as the two men shook hands.

Sheriff Morgan escorted the couple through the office area where each of the deputies rose to say their good-byes, Tom acknowledging them with handshakes and Betty speaking heartfelt words of appreciation.

At the door, Morgan spoke to Tom: "Once we catch these scalawags and bring 'em to trial, you'll need to testify."

"Be my duty and my pleasure, Sheriff."

Morgan took Betty's hand in both of his. "You have a safe trip home."

"Thank you, Sheriff. You've been a kind and considerate man."

Morgan gave a snort of laughter. "God Almighty, lady. Folks get that kind and considerate notion about me here in Placerville, that'll make it even badder than Sodom and Gomorrah."

Chapter Twenty-four

One man was riding out fast from the dilapidated split-log ranch house nestled in the hollow of the rolling foothills. Jed had been to this hideout building only once before and now he worried if he should have come at all. The man's frantic approach raised his own fears to an even higher level as the rider sped past.

He spurred his father's gelding to a gallop, vaulting from the horse in the yard before it came to a stop, and wrapping the reins to a hitching rail. Two other outlaws were in the yard, lifting saddles onto their mounts, their hasty actions signifying a harried departure. A horse harnessed to a buggy stood at the side of the house.

"Carl in there?" Jed shouted. "He still here?"

"In there," the towheaded young man answered. "Not for long."

184

Jed trotted to the door, opened it and walked in. Carl Parrish was at a table in the center of the main room, packing a suitcase with his fancy clothes. This was the first time Jed had seen the big man in workday denim jeans and a plaid shirt, as common in appearance as the other men who were gathering their belongings.

"You pulling out, Carl?" Jed exclaimed.

The big man gave him a withering look. "Everybody's pulling, Bill just left. I should have gone a couple of hours ago. Ross did soon as he heard." He paused. "Smarter than me."

"You see that damned paper? That Patterson bastard has done it for all of us. If I could kill that meddling—"

"We dealt the hand," Parrish cut in as he closed his suitcase. "Patterson played the aces. Game's over."

"I've lost everything . . . everything."

"So did the rest of us."

"What are we going to do?" Jed asked in desperation. "Ain't there something you or Mr. Sherwood can do?"

"Every man for himself."

"Where can I go?"

"Take off, kid," Parrish muttered and hoisted the suitcase. "Head for Mexico."

"That where you're going?"

"Maybe."

"Take me with you."

"Get away from me," Parrish said as he walked to the door. "No one in my buggy but me."

"You've got to take me! I don't know what to do."

"I ain't your momma, little boy. I'm aiming to move fast and that don't include showing you which way to run."

"I won't be any—"

The distant reports of two gunshots brought silence and dismay to the cabin room.

"What's that?" Jed asked even as he knew.

"That damned Ross gave us up," Parrish muttered. "We're smoked, boys."

Outside, the two men swung up onto their horses and, with shouts of alarm and bellowed curses, they galloped their mounts out of the yard, the pounding of the horse hooves diminishing as the two rode up the lane. Again, there were gunshots, nearer now, and a few seconds later the hoofbeat sounds of a returning horse thundered.

The towheaded cowboy burst through the front door, his boyish face contorted with fright and desperation, his breath coming in gasps. "Posse, Carl," he wheezed. "Big one, coming in on us."

"Heard shots, Johnny," Parrish said. "They shoot Ernie?"

The hard-breathing outlaw shook his head. "Fired warning shots, Ernie's going in with his hands up."

"I ain't giving myself up," growled one of the other men in the room. "We'll fight our way out."

"Too many," the towhead, Johnny, countered heatedly. "Maybe eighteen, twenty men out there."

"Been in jail before," Parrish muttered. "I'd rather fight than go in ever again."

"Can we give ourselves up, Carl?" another outlaw pleaded.

"We need your gun, Paulie," Parrish said grimly.

"I don't want to get killed," Paulie responded.

"Stay and fight or I'll backshoot you once you go out that door. You know I will."

Paulie stared hard. "I guess I do know that. You watch your own backsides."

Parrish shrugged. "Pick yourselves some shooting spots . . . at the windows here and that door in the back. These walls give pretty good cover."

"What do I do?" Jed asked.

"Try to keep from getting your head shot off," Parrish said. "Hold your shots 'til they come in close."

For ten minutes, the men in the ranch house stood guard at the front and rear openings of the building. Parrish, lying prone on the floor next to the front door, cracked it a few inches open and peered outside. "They're out of pistol range, using some boulders and a couple of trees for cover," he said. "How many rifles we got?"

"Two," came a reply. "Rest are in the saddles with the horses in the barn."

"Give me one," Carl commanded. "I'm good with a rifle."

"Good?" Jed exclaimed. "Maybe at shooting something as big as a horse."

Parrish ignored him. "Slide that rifle over to me," he ordered. After a moment's hesitation, one of the outlaws slid a rifle across the stone floor. Parrish examined the weapon, checked the load and moved to peer out the door once again.

"In the house!" came a cry from the yard. "This is Sheriff Morgan! You're surrounded! Come on out with your hands high and no guns! Come on out! You may do some time, but you'll have some living left! Stay and you'll die today, that's the way it is!"

Parrish poked the rifle barrel over the doorsill, sighted and fired at the top of a tall crowned hat bobbing sporadically into view above a large boulder. As the bullet cracked against stone, the hat ducked down.

"I 'spect that means you need some persuading!" Morgan's voice bellowed after a few moments.

From an arc of hidden shooters, a salvo of rifle shots began; a crackling overlay of repeating cartridge explosions accompanied by the whistling, thudding and crashing of bullets blasting onto and into the house. The stutter of gunfire was all around the house, shots coming at the front, sides and rear of the building. The horse hitched to the buggy bolted, the carriage bouncing crazily as it was hauled along the road to disappear in a cloud of dust. At the front hitching rail, the two tethered horses shied and whinnied and yanked repeatedly at their reins in their terror but, miraculously, remained unharmed.

The firing stopped abruptly.

"Anybody want to change their minds?" Morgan called.

"Anybody hurt?" Parrish asked, looking around.

No one answered.

"We ain't got a chance, Carl," Paulie said. "We're outgunned. They'll just sit there and keep shooting 'til we're done for."

Parrish didn't respond.

"What are we going to do?" asked another outlaw.

"Paulie's right," Parrish said after a long silence. "Stay here and they'll pick us off in their own sweet time." He paused. "We're going out the back to the horses."

"They're out there too!" Jed complained.

"Maybe not as many as in front," Parrish countered. He got up to his knees and crawled across the floor to the kitchen of the house and waved the others to crawl to him. "We go out in a rush shooting . . . shooting at everything in our way. We take our chances, everybody's on their own once they're out. Shoot at everything, jump on a horse and get the hell out of here."

"You ain't got a horse, Carl," Paulie growled. "You got nothing but a horse and a rig."

"Probably won't make it anyway," Parrish told him. "Not all of us going to get out of here alive so there's likely going to be a horse or two to spare."

"My horse is out front!" Jed exclaimed in panic.

"Mine too," said the towheaded young man.

"Let's do 'er now," Parrish commanded as he rose to a crouch. "Give 'em hell, boys!"

Three men followed Parrish out the back door of the house, breaking into a full run with revolvers blasting wildly as they dashed toward the barn.

"They're going out the back!" came a shout from a posse member. "Trying to get to the horses!"

Two of the fleeing men, one of them Parrish, reached the entrance to the barn unharmed. Paulie crumpled to the ground while the lanky man, Tim, mortally wounded, kept running and died on his feet before tumbling into the dirt.

Jed and the towhead, Johnny, remained on the kitchen floor, looking out the door, transfixed by the sight. They could hear other posse members coming around the house, a number of them converging on the action. They saw flashes from guns from inside the shadowed barn as the two men blasted back at their hunters. Suddenly, Parrish on horseback bolted out of the barn, the animal whipped to full gallop while the rider lay low against the horse's neck. A volley of shots from in front frightened the horse and it reared to a stop, forelegs flailing.

"Out the front!" Jed barked to the young man beside him. "Make a run for it!" He leaped to his feet and saw, in a fleeting glance over his shoulder, Parrish's body being riddled with bullets, the final volley slamming him out of the saddle and to the ground.

Johnny went out the front door first with Jed staying close behind him. Two shots whizzed close as they ran to the hitching rail. Jed's horse was alone, the other gone.

"Mine's gone!" the young man cried out in terror.

"Drop your guns!" shouted a voice. "You're covered!"

Jed acted quickly to holster his revolver and wrap an arm around his companion's neck, the move surprising and alarming the young man.

"What the hell—"

"Shut up, I'm getting out of here," Jed muttered, his free hand unwrapping the reins of his horse from the rail.

"Give it up, Jed!" The deputy, Nick, rose from his concealment as did three other posse members. "You can't get away."

Using the outlaw as a shield, Jed moved to the saddle, then drew his revolver and began firing. Nick and the posse members, anticipating, dropped into cover once again and returned fire.

Jed felt the thud of the two separate bullets that kicked Johnny's body back into him. He heard the young man's sharp intake of a final breath as he flung the dying man away and vaulted onto the horse's back. He dug his spurs frantically, letting the horse run wildly, hearing the shots fired and the buzzing of bullets whipping inches close as he rode for his life. The horse was running at full speed into the mountainous terrain, Jed hanging on.

A bullet ticked his shoulder and another grazed the side of his head. He laid his head against the horse's neck and dug the rowels into the flanks again and again.

Ten minutes later, he exulted in triumph. He had outrun death, he had survived, he was alive!

As he slowed his horse to a panting walk, he looked

back and could see no sign of pursuit. "They'll pay, God damn it," he muttered. "They'll pay."

Sheriff Morgan watched as two of his posse members rode up the lane with the shackled prisoner on horseback between them. He joined his two deputies as they and others walked around the yard, inspecting the still bodies, looking for and finding no life left in any one of them.

"It's the job," Nick said to him. "But I don't like it."

"They had the choice," Morgan reminded him. "Lucky none of us was hit."

"I know," Nick agreed. "Still wish they'd given up."

"Bad men come to bad ends," the sheriff said.

"You read that somewhere or just make it up?" Nick asked with a slight smile.

"Kinda got a ring to it, don't it?"

"Young Porter got away," Mitch ventured. "Rode out there in the hills, bullets chasing him."

"Maybe one got him," Morgan said.

Mitch shook his head. "I think he got clear."

"Well, we'll catch up to him later," the sheriff said.

"Funny thing," his chief deputy said, looking into the mountains. "Young Porter chased Patterson into them hills and now he's on the run up there."

"Sling them bodies over whatever horses you find," Morgan said. "Get 'em back to town for burying."

Chapter Twenty-five

Langdon Sherwood took the tickets from his inside coat pocket, looked at them and then laid them to one side on his desk. One was for a solo train trip to San Francisco on the morrow and the other for a single passage on a steamship leaving the day after for South America. The stopover in the city would give him ample time to arrange a transfer of more than fifteen million dollars of investors' money he had, wisely and surreptitiously, deposited in his own account rather than placed as promised in escrow.

Nonetheless, a note to those investors was necessary, a tactic to delay any legal actions until he was well out of reach in a country with no reciprocal extradition agreements. He returned his attention to what he was writing, considering his next sentence, his pen poised

over his expensive monogrammed stationary. He nodded, congratulating himself for clear thinking, then
dipped the nib in the inkwell and began to write, saying
the words aloud as he formed them on the paper.

"We are pleased to advise you that our land acquisi-
tion efforts are entering a highly satisfactory and final
phase. We wish to assure you and our other esteemed
venture investors that we anticipate a public announce-
ment and the start of actual construction possibly in the
summer of next year."

"Some gentlemen to see you, Langdon," said the
gaunt woman in the doorway of his study. She was a
plain person in plain clothing, a drab contradiction to
her peacock of a husband.

Sherwood stopped writing, blotted the ink on the
paper, and leaned back from his rolltop desk, his reading glasses dropping from his nose to dangle on a cord
from his vest. "Mildred, I've asked you over and over
not to bother me when I'm working."

"They say they are with the police," his wife responded with just the slightest suggestion of a smirk on
her pale, pinched face.

Sherwood gave no indication of alarm. "The police?
Well, then, show them in, my dear." He slid the two
tickets under a book on the desk.

Mildred Sherwood walked out of sight and, a few
moments later, returned with two middle-aged men,
bowler hats in hand, their eyes roving over the sumptu-
ous furnishings of the stately house interior. Both were

robust men, unaccustomed to and uncomfortable in the cheap suits they wore.

"You may leave us, Mildred," Sherwood said, not bothering to rise to greet his visitors.

"I'll stay," his wife responded flatly. "I think I've waited a long time for this."

Sherwood's eyes widened in fury.

"Mr. Sherwood," one of the men began. "I'm Detective Anderson. This is my partner, Detective O'Malley. We have a warrant for your arrest, sir." So saying, Anderson took a document from his inside coat pocket. "If you'll come along quietly—"

"Arrest?" Sherwood exploded. "For what?"

"You're being charged with a number of counts of fraud and, more important, as a conspirator and accessory in the murders of Edward Portee and Ezekiel Hamilton," Anderson said.

"This is preposterous. Out of my house immediately!" the diminutive attorney bellowed as he sprang to his feet, his short stature presenting a comic tableau between the two towering men. "Your warrant be damned. I'm not guilty of anything. I'm a respected attorney and I'll have your jobs for this!"

Detective Anderson sighed and nodded to his companion. Immediately, the second policeman moved to pin Sherwood's arms behind him with one hand, his other fishing handcuffs from a pocket.

"Stop this!" Sherwood shouted, trying to pull away. "You stupid lout! Get your hands off of me!"

Seconds later, the big policeman stepped away as the lawyer continued to struggle against the shackles, his protests and swear words diminishing into mutterings and gasps as he tugged to free himself.

"Sorry, ma'am," Detective Anderson turned to the silent woman. "I know this must be unpleasant for you."

Mildred Sherwood's dour face broke into a wide and joyous smile. "Unpleasant? Unpleasant?" she crowed. "Take him away and good riddance to him! I've waited for years for a moment like this to happen!"

In wonderment and some amusement, the two detectives dragged the struggling, kicking and now sobbing lawyer between them to the door where Mildred Sherwood rushed to open it for them.

Chapter Twenty-six

Jed Porter's sharp Spanish rowels dug again and again at the fresh bloody wounds on the horse's flanks, but the animal refused to take more than a few steps and stopped again. Disgusted and swearing, Jed dismounted, took his rifle from the saddle scabbard and contemplated shooting the horse. He looked around at the bleak Nevada landscape, hoping to see a ranch or a small settlement but the horizon was as empty and desolate as the arid land at his feet.

He was tired and worn and, with a small measure of grudging awareness, he knew his horse was exhausted. After his escape from the posse, he had ridden the animal hard, feeling the strength of his mount lessening mile after mile. He had crossed into Nevada and started south, an idea of Mexico as a refuge in his mind. He glanced quickly at the sun and determined the hour as mid-afternoon. If he didn't find shelter, he would have to spend the night in the open and he flinched at that thought. He began to walk and, to his surprise, his horse followed. "Stay out here and die, you damned nag," he said aloud. "What good are you?"

For an hour he trudged on, his eyes scanning the ground at each step, fearing rattlesnakes hidden under the sagebrush. His horse continued to follow, pausing for long periods of time and catching up with a sporadic trotting gait.

As he came to the top of a gentle rise, he was elated at the sight of a line of trees bordering each side of a desert stream with a long swale of green grass and foliage on the banks. In the near distance, he could see a tiny house, a weathered barn and two horses moving slowly in a corral.

He walked back to his horse and took the reins in his hand. He started to remount and then reconsidered. Instead, he led the horse as he walked toward the ranch oasis.

Fifteen minutes later, he entered the yard of the humble dwelling, walked past the corral with an appraising eye on the two horses. One was a decent animal with good lines, a gray mare he judged no more than four or five years of age. The other horse, a sway-backed skewbald, was an old one.

As Jed approached the small house, the screen door

opened and a portly, middle-aged Mexican man with a rifle stepped out, the weapon held chest high.

"Hold on there, pard!" Jed called and laid his own rifle on the ground and held his hands above his head. "I'm lost and my horse is wore out!"

The two men stood still.

"You speak English?" Jed asked.

The Mexican nodded.

"All I'm looking for is a drink of water and some shade to rest in. That's all I'm asking."

"Why you here?"

"Like I said . . . lost my way."

"Pistol too!"

Jed smiled and, with two fingers, removed the revolver from his holster and lowered it toward the ground. Then, his hand curled around the grip and his index finger sought the trigger. He raised the weapon and fired three times.

The rifle dropped from the man's hands and he fell back against the screen door. With a low moan, his upper body slid to the side and he lay with open, unseeing eyes against the siding. There was a scream from inside the house and a slight, mature Mexican woman came to the door, hysterical and shrieking in terror.

"Damn," Jed muttered. He aimed and shot twice through the screen door.

Afterward, he walked through the cluttered little home and searched the outer buildings to make sure there were no others to kill. He dragged both bodies into the barn and laid them side by side in one of the stalls.

Place to stay for a couple of days, maybe a week, he considered as he walked to the house. *Move on to Mexico or, maybe not. For the mess I'm in, there's a man to blame, a score to settle.*

He entered the modest home and found the couple's evening meal warm on the back of the kitchen stove. He took a plate from one of the cabinets and spooned a generous helping of a savory beef stew onto it.

Chapter Twenty-seven

"**Y**eah, I got the wire," Marshal Judd muttered in response to Tom's question and nodded to the telegram sheet on the desk in front of him. "You didn't need to come see me."

"I wanted to make sure," Tom said forcefully. "No mistakes and you saying 'I didn't know.'"

"Okay, okay, you're clear," Judd acknowledged, his vexation apparent. "You got no call to brace me. It ain't that I'd up and shoot you for no reason at all. I *am* the law here, you know."

"That ain't saying much," Tom countered. He picked up the letter from the desk and turned to the elderly jailer, Luke, and a pimple-faced young man named Ned who served as the marshal's only deputy. "You boys are witnesses to what the marshal is saying. This letter and the telegram from Sheriff Morgan over there in Placerville cancels out any warrant for me and clears me of all charges."

The old jailer and the young deputy nodded their agreement.

"Now," Tom turned his steady gaze back on the marshal, "when you was talking with my wife while I was gone, I hear you was making some comments about putting a hurt on her."

The obese lawman squirmed under the fierce look of Tom's eyes. "I surely regret that. I spoke out of turn. I didn't really mean anything bad to your lady."

"Not the way I heard it."

"I'm sorry, that's all I can say."

Tom regarded him for a few long seconds. "Judd, this ain't a big town and I reckon the law don't need much more than you to handle it right now. When we get bigger, we're going to need somebody who knows what the hell they're doing and that surely ain't you. You best find some other way to earn your vittles." He turned and walked to the door. "You see me on the street, you move to the other side." He opened the door and walked out.

He turned to stride along the boardwalk, a joyful sense of relief in his heart and mind, thankful the ordeal was at an end. He nodded and spoke pleasantly to the men and women he met as he walked toward the stable, noting with satisfaction that the residents of Red Cliff greeted him with smiles and murmurs of congratulations. *By darn! I guess I'm a bit of a hero!*

Chuckling at his vanity, he walked into the large, opened doors of the stable and entered the office partition where Betty was visiting with Bert Stevens.

"There you are," Betty greeted him. "Where have you been?"

"Down at the marshal's office. Making sure Judd knew all charges had been dropped."

She looked at him closely. "It wasn't about what he said to me?"

"Some."

"I shouldn't have even told you," she said in a mild rebuke. "Wasn't nothing for you to fuss about."

"No fuss. Just reminding him to watch his mouth talking to ladies."

"Bert and I were talking about us buying the stable," she said with a glance to the older man at his desk. "He's giving us a good price."

"I'll throw in the rig rental business in the same deal," Stevens said. "Livestock too."

"That mean you're getting out of business all together?" Tom asked.

Stevens nodded. "Got some money saved up and what with them payments you're making now and a little bit more for the building, I can do the rest of my days okay."

"It's been nice having you here to watch things while we're on the road," Tom said. "You still want to do that?"

Stevens shook his head. "Nope, when I'm done, I'm done."

"Uncle Willie can handle the in and outs on the rentals," Betty said. "I'll keep an eye on him and the books."

"Sure," Stevens agreed. "Willie is smart enough when you lay out what he's to do."

Tom knew the rig rental business was a minimal endeavor that didn't require much attention. Nonetheless, he said, "I'll have to hire another helper for the big loads."

"There's plenty of good young 'uns looking for work," Betty told him. "You've said so yourself."

Tom nodded, a sign of consent. "Sound good to me. We'll get that lawyer fellow to draw up what papers we need to deal."

"Speaking of lawyers, you see about little Mr. Sherwood," Betty asked, a satisfied smile on her face. "In today's paper, he's been . . . what they call *indicted*. Probably going to be in prison the rest of his life."

Tom returned the smile. "Hadn't heard, but that's good news." His face sobered. "Nothing about young Porter?"

Betty shook her head. "On the run. Maybe down in Mexico."

"Shame. Parrish paid for his killing, but Jed ain't yet paid for his."

A silence lasted for a long period of time.

"You've got a run tomorrow to Auburn to meet the train," Betty said, bringing up a new topic. "I'm trying to find a load going but you may have to deadhead if I can't." She took a shipment order from a small pile on a table and handed it to Tom. "Fifteen cast-iron cook-stoves coming in from St. Louis. Station master will have 'em in a boxcar on a siding."

"They coming here?" Tom asked, looking at the bill of lading and answering his own question. "I see that they come to our hardware store." He looked up at his wife. "Lordy, old man Crawford thinks he can sell fifteen stoves?"

"New folks coming in all the time," Betty replied. "Selling 'em ain't our problem. Just make sure he pays for our hauling on delivery."

"Be gone overnight," Tom estimated. "Some of the afternoon and the next morning to load 'em. Include a couple of hotel rooms and eats on the bill, Bett." He sighed. "Good Lord, cast-iron cook stoves."

Bert gave a sudden cackle. "Heavy lifting, Thomas. Don't throw your back out like I did mine."

Tom nodded and grinned. "Get as old and worn out as you, Bert, I'll sell the outfit to somebody stupid as me, you betcha."

Betty rose from her chair. "I'm heading over to the Wilson house. I heard they was getting ready to move to Auburn. Maybe we could give 'em a good price on sending some of their furniture ahead."

"I'll walk with you," Tom said.

"Be better if you'd go a different direction and scare up some other load to put on that big wagon," she admonished him.

"We'll talk about it," he replied.

They said their good-byes to Bert and moved out into the sunlight and walked side by side along the boardwalk.

"You getting too old for that lifting?" Betty asked.

"Naw, I'm fine. Don't worry about me."

She walked in silence for another minute. "I do worry," she said suddenly.

"About my lifting?"

She shook her head and looked down as she stepped along. "It's silly. I keep hoping they'll catch that Porter kid."

"Hell, he's down south of the border by now. You think he'd come after you and me?"

She nodded.

"He shows his face anywhere in these United States and he's a goner. They'll clap him in jail and hang him soon as a jury gives an okay."

"I'll be a lot happier when that happens," she told him. "What he did to that old man at his ranch was bad. It was mean and from what you told me, probably wasn't even necessary."

"They'll catch him one of these days," he reassured her. "He's running from the law and, some place, some day, they'll catch him."

"They didn't catch you."

Tom pulled a comical face. "Yeah, but he ain't nearly as smart as me."

She nodded and tucked her arm in his. "And, pity

sakes, no *really* smart wife to pull *his* chestnuts out of the fire."

Sharing laughter and then an ardent embrace, Mr. and Mrs. Patterson raised eyebrows on the main street of their hometown.

Chapter Twenty-eight

"Y̶ou feel as foolish as I do?" Tom asked.

George Martinez nodded, a sheepish grin on his face. "Good thing we got the tarp," he said, glancing over his shoulder at the jumble of different-height shapes under the gray-green tarpaulin occupying a lesser section of the large wagon. One unseen article of considerable size and height formed the apex of the tented canvas that cloaked the cargo. They were four miles out of Red Cliff and the team of big Belgian horses was plodding at the normal unhurried pace, Ginger and George's horses tethered to and trailing the wagon.

"Get the danged thing delivered after sundown," Tom growled, snapping the reins to goad the team to pull against the rising grade in the road. "It surely is grounds for getting unhitched."

"Divorce?" George laughed.

"Have me one of those in a minute," Tom said. "Judge would say it was a cruel and terrible thing she done to me. And her laughing at me all the time we was loading."

"The Patterson Freight Company." George continued to chuckle. "Privy moving our specialty."

"Danged wind comes along and blows off the tarp in town, we'd be the laughingstock." He shook his head. "She ought not have taken this load."

"Hell, Tom, it ain't like it's ever been used. That Mr. Wilson spent a lot of time building this new one. It's got them smooth edged holes and those fancy stars and a crescent moon in the door. All real pretty. It's a work of art."

"I wouldn't have put it past Betty to give him a deal transporting the old one . . . with Wilson sitting right in there next to a box of corn cobs."

"Well, you can see why he wanted to take it to where he's moving," George persisted. "No one really wants to buy a place with somebody else's outhouse."

"Let's change the subject," Tom suggested. "How's new married life?"

"Doing fine," said his helper with a prideful smile. "Me and Emmy Sue just as happy as we can be."

Jed Porter dismounted from his horse and, with an appraising glance at the small town, entered the front door of the café. The café was a narrow facility with two

rows of three tables against opposite walls. The only pa-
tron sitting at one table on the left was picking at a plate
of food and sipping coffee from a mug. An open kitchen
with a cook working at the rear brought both the pungent smell of cooking and a considerable amount of
heat to the dining room. The one waitress, heavyset and
middle-aged, had beads of sweat on her florid face.

As way of a disguise, he wore a full beard and dark
denim clothing, an effect that made him appear older.
He seated himself at a table on the right side at the back
of the room, facing the entrance. "Am I too late for
lunch?" he asked the waitress.

"Guess not," she said irritably. "You'll have to make
do with what's left, we ain't going to cook special for
you."

"Okay," Jed agreed pleasantly. "Just a little hungry.
Anything will do."

"I'll see if I've got something good left," the woman
said, modifying her tone.

"Question before you do," he said quickly. "Fellow
named Tom Patterson . . . he lives here in town?"

"Yeah, that's right. Kinda half-famous these days, I
suppose you know."

Jed shrugged as if he didn't.

"Well, some bad stuff went on over in Placerville,"
she said and gave him a questioning look. "What you
want with him?"

"Looking for work, I guess. Heard they had a freight
business. I'm kinda down on my luck."

The woman looked him up and down. "You *do* look a bit scrawny for that kind of hard work. You might try over at the livery stable, talk to Tom or his missus."

"I'll do that . . . and thank you."

"I'll see what I can round up for you," she said and walked into the kitchen area.

While she was engaged in conversation with the cook, Jed rose from his chair and made his way quietly to the door, opened it and closed it softly behind him as he walked out.

The woman turned, a plate of food in her hand, and looked with surprise at the empty chair at the table, her eyes flashing to the front window in search of the young man. He was nowhere in sight. "Well, if that don't beat all," she said aloud. "Teach me to feel sorry for some saddlebum."

The door opened again and Marshal Judd walked in, his eyes immediately fastening on the plate in the waitress' hand. He moved to a table, pulled a chair way back to accommodate his girth and sat down heavily. "Coffee, I guess, Maxine," he muttered.

"You want this food?" the woman asked, knowing the answer.

"Who was it for?"

"Young fellow came in, said he was hungry . . . I turned around and he was gone."

Judd nodded. "Seen him on the way out." He pointed a finger at the food plate. "Don't reckon that ought to go to waste."

The waitress placed the plate in front of him, half-turned away and then turned back. "Something about that young guy. He was asking about Tom Patterson."

"Probably wanted to go pay his respects to our hero," Judd said sarcastically, his fork already stabbing into a sausage patty.

"Tom made some enemies over there. Maybe you ought to go check that young man out."

Judd shook his head, his mouth full as he answered. "Ain't none of my concern who or whatever he is."

She arched her eyebrows and turned away. "I'll get you that coffee."

Jed walked along the street leading his horse, his eyes fastened on the livery stable ahead. He wrapped the reins at a hitching rail across from the barn and stepped into the deep shade between two buildings, standing far enough away from the street that he would not be easily seen by anyone at the stable. He sat down against a building wall, lolling his head in an intoxicated pose; he would likely be mistaken for a mid-afternoon drunk if seen by any passerby. He drew the revolver from beneath his jacket and twirled the cylinder to confirm a full load. Satisfied, still gripping it, he laid it in his lap, ready to bring it up instantly.

For several minutes, he could see no activity at the stable. Then, an attractive blond woman came out of the door accompanied by two men, one late middle-aged, the other elderly. *Likely Mrs. Patterson*, he reasoned. *A chance to hurt Patterson better than any other way!*

He raised the revolver and rolled onto his stomach, a prone position to take aim. He planted both elbows on the ground, his arms formed in a steady inverted V. He lined the front sight of the revolver with the woman's body and started finger pressure on the trigger.

Across the street, the elderly man stepped to a different position and blocked his angle. "Move, you old turkey," Jed exclaimed in a whisper as he relaxed his trigger finger. "Get out of the way."

The trio on the other side of the street continued their conversation, the old man shifting from side to side, giving Jed tantalizing yet fleeting chances at his target.

Then, they separated, the woman walking quickly away—too quickly—and the two men returned to the interior of the stable. Jed rose and hurried to the corner of the building, his revolver held low, peeking around the building edge to regain his sight of the woman. *Too far! Out of my range!*

He concealed the Colt under his jacket and walked across the street to the stable. He peered into the shadowed interior of the barn both relieved and frustrated not to see Tom Patterson. Still being careful, he walked into the barn and moved cautiously to the open door of the small office—Patterson was not inside, only the two older men.

"Help you?" the elderly man asked.

"I was hoping to see Mr. Patterson," Jed said in a fawning manner. "Looking for work. Is he hiring?"

"Can't say," the old man answered. "He's out of town for a couple of days, maybe three."

"Is that so?" Jed said as a question. "Over to Sacramento?"

"Naw, he ain't," the other man blurted. "He and George are gone to Auburn."

"Uncle Willie!" the elderly man said sharply.

"I'll try to see him when he gets back," Jed said in his most polite way. He turned and walked several feet out of sight, then paused.

"Uncle Willie," the old man was lecturing. "You hadn't ought to say things when you shouldn't. Don't go telling things to strangers. None of that fellow's business."

"Sorry, Bert," came a subdued response. "I surely won't ever again."

Jed stepped out into the sunlight. Down the street, he saw the Patterson woman crossing the street on her way to the dry goods store. *Too far away, too many people. After I take care of him, maybe I'll drop by on another day.*

He walked the short distance to his horse, swung up into the saddle, and spurred the horse on the road to Auburn.

Chapter Twenty-nine

The long wagon was positioned next to the open door of the boxcar where he and George had wrestled the heavy wooden crates, each stamped with the shipper's name, Majestic Manufacturing Company.

"That's the last one." Tom sighed his relief as they positioned the final crate on the wagon. "Fifteen iron cookstoves all the way from St. Looie, Missouri."

George sat on one of the crates and wiped the sweat from his forehead with the sleeve of his shirt. "Maybe me and Emmy Sue might be buying one of 'em ourselves soon as we can find a place of our own." He gave a rueful smile. "Ain't much fun living in her folk's spare room."

"That old man, Eli Wheeler, ain't looking too spry these days," Tom said. "I 'spect his place might be vacant any day now."

215

"No kin?"

"Nope. It ain't much to look at, but you could probably get it from the bank for what he still owes on it and you could fix it up. Make it into a cozy little place to set up your housekeeping."

"That's a thought, Tom. Reckon the banker would be agreeable?"

"Might if I was to back your play."

"I'd appreciate that a whole lot."

"Let's get on our way home," Tom said. He jumped down from the wagon and walked across the tracks of two spur lines to the shade of a nearby poplar where George's horse and his Ginger were tethered. He took the reins of both animals and led them back to tie them to the rear end of the long wagon, then trotted to join George waiting beside the Belgian team at the front.

Three hundred feet away, behind the cover of a rail yard utility shed, Jed Porter watched the two men climb up onto the front seat of the wagon and start the sturdy team on a slow, heavy-burdened journey. He could have picked off Patterson at any time in the past hour and had considered doing so several times, but the railroad center was far too busy with too many people to call an alarm or even interfere. In fact, on two occasions, railroad workers had stared, obviously wondering what he was doing loitering at a railroad workplace. A killing here in town would likely result in his capture or, even worse, his own death.

He strolled unhurriedly to his horse and swung up onto the saddle. He waited until the huge wagon moved out of the rail yard, then spurred his mount into a dawdling pace to follow. He kept well back of the slow moving wagon, reining his horse to a stop several times to keep from overtaking it as it passed through the cross streets of the industrial area.

At the edge of town, he stopped his horse again and watched as the big wagon lumbered on the road to Red Cliff. He stroked the walnut stock of the rifle with almost a caress, longing to draw it even now.

"Later," he said aloud. "Out in the lonesome."

He waited and watched until the wagon had diminished to a tiny speck in the distance, then spurred his horse to move ahead on the road. Earlier, on his way toward Auburn, he had selected a pair of promising positions for an ambush. His optimum choice was three miles ahead of the wagon, a passageway between two rounded hills with trees and scrub brush at the summits to provide ample cover for a rifleman at top of either and no protection for those on the road. No large rocks or trees or even large shrubs existed on the brown landscape the road traveled before it reached the small pass. It was a perfect killing field, the very place for revenge.

Slashing the rein ends at the withers and digging his heels into the flanks, he spurred the horse into a gallop and then veered into the hilly countryside, circling far left in a wide arc that would take him well ahead of the wagon, to wait in that place of final opportunity.

The draft horse team, Clyde and Claude, pulled the heavy load steadily, the strength of the Belgians ever a source of amazement even to the two men who well knew the incredible might of the animals. The pace was not fast, but it was a constant and satisfying progress. From their high seat above and behind the team, Tom and George viewed the sinewy musculatures of the thick necks and broad backs as the horses matched in unison their short strides, their heads bowed as they plodded powerfully onward. Behind the two men, the fifteen crated stoves rode in the wagon bed and, by their weight, remained solidly unmoved by the bumps and rolls of the rutted road under the high wheels.

As they rounded a bend in the road to a straightaway, George made a slight cough, an indication that he was about to speak. "Maybe it's my imagination," he said.

Tom waited.

"Awhile back, way off to our left—"

"A rider," Tom interposed. "Maybe just some cowboy working the area."

George nodded.

"Or maybe not," Tom speculated. "Caught a glimpse of him riding fast through a cut over there in the hills."

"What are you thinking?"

"Like maybe he was swinging wide to get ahead of us."

George pursed his lips and furrowed his brow. "If he's the robbing sort, I don't think he'd want to carry off cookstoves."

"Maybe he just wants to say 'Howdy,'" Tom suggested and nodded his head to the considerable distance where the road passed between two hills. "Like maybe just right up there ahead in that gap."

"Some leftover business from over there in Placerville?"

Tom shrugged. "Could be. Law's still looking for the young buck who got away. Might be him, might not."

George tugged on the reins and brought the team to a halt. "Saying 'howdy' might not be what he has in mind. Want to turn around?"

"You're a young fellow with a new bride," Tom told him. "Unhitch your horse and stay out of this . . . if there really is trouble."

"No, sir," George said vehemently. "You're not taking this wagon through that gap by yourself."

"Ain't your fight."

"I'm making it mine."

"I'm the boss," Tom said sharply. "Do as I say."

"Begging your pardon, Mr. Boss, I'm staying. You can fire me, but I ain't going to be known as a scaredy-cat in my own hometown." He glared his indignation. "You can put that in your damned pipe and smoke it."

Tom's face slowly broke into a sly grin. "Maybe

there ain't nobody up there to make all this fuss about anyways."

"And maybe there is."

Tom put his hand to his chin and stared straight ahead. After a few seconds, he turned to his helper. "Help me drag a couple of them small tarps we got in the wagon box. We'll prop 'em up here in the seats, put our hats on 'em, and keep the whole shebang heading into that gap."

"Where'll we be?"

"*You'll* be sitting back under cover between a couple of them iron cookstoves with the reins, guiding our rig on the road."

"And you?"

"I'll be riding Ginger and skirting around to come up on that hill, sorta like a surprise."

"Won't he see you?"

"We're still a far ways and, if he's really there, I'd guess he won't be looking at much other than our wagon," Tom said. "You bring the team along slow and easy and, when you get somewhere shy of rifle range, you stop and wait awhile."

" 'Til when?"

" 'Til I show myself and tell you it's all clear."

"You're taking all the chances, Tom."

Tom shook his head. "You're gonna be what we rebs called a diversion. Even if he's outta range, he may throw a few shots at the wagon. You stay in between them cast-iron stoves."

They moved onto the wagon bed and opened a large storage box behind the seat. They took out two of the smaller-sized rolled tarpaulins and propped them into the leg cavity of the driver's seat. They doffed their hats and placed one on top of each roll.

"Hope no breeze blows 'em off," George said.

"Just keep it going if it does."

"You going now?"

Tom nodded. "I'll drop off and lead my horse back to that bend before I get mounted. Give me a little bit of time, then start moving the rig toward that gap." He rolled out of the seat and dropped to the ground.

"Be careful!" George called as he sat down behind the storage box and between two crated stoves.

Tom led Ginger out of sight at the bend of the road. He heard George's sharp whistle and shout as he started the heavy horses on the journey again. He stepped into the stirrup and hoisted himself onto the saddle and nudged the horse first into a walk, then into a trot as he headed into the rough and uneven terrain. He bent low over the horse and kept its pace at no more than an occasional canter, wary that a dust trail might reveal his position. He covered the distance within a few minutes, occasionally glancing back to track the progress of the slow moving team and wagon.

Circling wide to the base of the hill on the left side of the road, Tom tugged Ginger to a stop, slipped from the saddle and placed the reins beneath a large stone. He looked around for a horse, assuming that Porter, if here, would have left his mount nearby. *Not here. Maybe somewhere else.*

He drew his rifle from the saddle scabbard, transferred it to his left hand and then drew his Colt Peacemaker with his right. Crouching low, he moved up the slope, feeling very vulnerable in the open without even a mound or a depression in to provide cover. He scurried to the crest of the hill and into the scant protection of an isolated pair of slender pine trees. Across a twenty-five-foot stretch of bare ground, a thicket of firs, pines and birch was a likely place for a rifleman.

He deliberated his next move. If he had been seen or heard in his dash up the hill, Porter would be in that grove waiting for the moment he stepped into the clearing. Caution argued for him to stay hidden, to listen for a sound and look for a movement. *Let Porter make the mistake.*

Tom glanced back at the road and saw the team and wagon slowly approaching. The illusion was convincing, Tom decided. From this distance, it appeared two bulky men with hats sat in the driver's seat. *Perhaps Porter's attention would be on the wagon. Make my play now!*

Tom leaped from behind the two pines and ran at full speed to the nearest large tree in the grove and reached it, no shots fired. Pressing his body against it, his eyes searched the section of the woods in which a shooter might have a line on him.

Nothing!

He dropped to one knee and laid his rifle on the ground, trusting his revolver as a more appropriate weapon for a close engagement. He stayed quiet and listened. Nothing moved in the woods, no twig snapped, no birds took sudden wing. Tom focused his gaze, sector by sector, exploring the grove of trees.

No one there!

Nonetheless, he moved cautiously through the grove, searching every niche, every depression in the ground.

No one there!

Standing behind a tree as a protection from a shot from the opposite hill, he looked back at the wagon that had stopped a long distance away. He looked down the road in the other direction and—he couldn't be sure—thought he could see a rider. A moment later, there was no one in sight and he wondered if he had seen anyone at all.

He retrieved his rifle and retraced his path down the hill and, chiding himself for foolishness, came to the road and sprinted to the other side. He explored it, forcing himself to repeat his caution and found this hill, too, unoccupied. He moved to the center of the road and waved for George to bring the wagon, then jogged to retrieve Ginger.

Jed continued to ride his horse at a gallop far past the possibility of pursuit. *It had been a close call,* he thought with bitterness and chagrin. *The trap for Patterson almost became mine!* A spiral of dust that might have been only a swirling wind had alerted him and the distant sight of only a single horse at the rear of the wagon had convinced him that Patterson had guessed him out. He had run at his instinctive alarm, swearing as he plunged down the hill to his horse. He leaped into the saddle and whipped the horse in a frenzy, digging his sharp rowels into the sides to goad the animal to a dangerous run over irregular ground. He had returned to the road only after the horse stumbled and, miraculously, recovered its stride. Looking back over his shoulder, the wagon was a tiny speck and there was no rider on horseback in pursuit. Nonetheless, he continued to whip and spur the horse to a full gallop.

Chapter Thirty

Late in the afternoon, Tom and George hoisted the last of the crates onto the loading dock behind the Crawford Hardware Store while the older Crawford and his two sons watched without helping. The job had been all the harder in that other crates and barrels of different stores had been left scattered in the narrow alley, too many bulky items to move to allow passage for Tom's big wagon. As a result, they'd unloaded the fifteen stoves from the wagon bed and, unable to dolly the crates on the muddy alleyway, hand carried each between them to the dock.

"Thanks, boys," the elder Crawford said as he entered the back door of his building followed by his two smirking sons.

"Reckon they'll stay out here 'til they're sold," George ventured.

Tom nodded. "Hope they rust before they sell." He pointed a finger at the horse team and wagon at the end of the alley. "Can you take the outfit on over to the stable and take care of the horses? Rub 'em down good, feed and water 'em?"

"Sure," George said. "Where you going?"

"Over to the blacksmith's and a couple of other places. Some things I gotta do."

"What'll I say to your missus?"

"That I'm going to be awhile. I'll be along as soon as I can."

"You going to tell her about what happened on our way back?"

"You mean what didn't happen. Yeah, you just might tell her to stay inside and not out onto the street."

"You worried that fellow might come looking for you here?"

"We don't know he was anywhere near. Maybe just our imagination."

"You're likely right about that. Man would be a damned fool to come here. He'd be smarter to get clean out of California."

"You never know about people with a grudge," Tom philosophized. "They don't always do the smart things."

In the early night darkness, Jed lay on his belly behind a slight knoll in the vacant lot diagonally across the street from the Patterson house. Several lamps were lit in the dwelling and, once, the man himself had stood momentarily in the doorway, not long enough for Jed to fire a shot. He had seen him twice more through the front window as he had moved swiftly across the living room.

On a couple of occasions, he had heard Patterson's voice loudly joking with his wife, the words not quite clear, but the man was obviously in a good mood. *Laugh while you can, dead man!*

At last, Jed's patience was rewarded. Patterson appeared once more in the doorway, a dark silhouette against the backlight in the house. "All right, come out when you're done!" Patterson called. "I'll be taking my pipe!"

Jed took careful aim and tracked Patterson as he walked across the porch and sat down in a porch glider. The angle was good even over the waist-high wooden porch wall that skirted the enclosure—a clear view of the dark outlined head, chest and shoulders. He lined the front sight of the rifle on Patterson's chest and curled his finger against the trigger, then relaxed it as the man bent down, reaching for something on the floor. Seconds later, he rose again and started the glider swinging back and forth, back and forth.

Jed's first shot was true, the bullet dead on target, the jolt of the impact slamming the body and propelling the glider back on the porch. A tremendous cry of pain wailed from the porch. Exulted, Jed aimed again—his second, third and fourth shots following in rapid succession, at least two more striking the flailing Patterson before he fell to the floor.

Jed couldn't restrain his cry of wordless jubilation as he leaped to his feet and began running through the backyards of the neighborhood houses. Behind him, he heard a woman's scream and his elation soared. He sprinted across the vacant ground to a grove of trees where he had tied his horse. He untied the reins, stepped up into the stirrup and pulled himself up onto the saddle. With a jab of his spurs, he prodded his horse into a trot and headed for the center of the town.

Should've done the woman as well. Should have shot them both right there in their cozy little house. He immediately dismissed his thought. "Got even," he said aloud. "Did I ever!"

"Good scream," Tom said from the floor of the porch. "He's gone, but you stay in the house all the same."

"You fool!" Betty fussed. "I should never have let you do such a dumb stunt!"

Tom rose from the floor and looked at the shattered mannequin that lay under the glider. "Gonna have to pay Harper's Ready-to-Wear for their store dummy. Ain't much left of it." He chuckled. "Sat down, bent down, then pushed the dummy up and put it to swinging. Must've pulled the wool over his eyes . . . he sure blasted the hell out of it."

"Could've been you, you blockhead," Betty continued as she edged out onto the porch. "You sure he's gone?"

"Yep, peeked over and saw him hightailing it across the back lots."

"Well, what good was all this?" she complained and then looked out into the street. "Here come the neighbors."

"We put on a good show, didn't we?" Tom asked and unbuttoned his shirt. "Help me get this rig off. Damn, it's heavy."

Betty took his shirt while he ducked his head down and slipped under one of the two straps that joined two foot-wide iron plates that had hung low over his chest and back. "Got this idea when we was carrying them iron stoves," he told her. "I told George them stoves would protect him from gunfire." He chortled at his own cleverness. "Went over to the smithy, told him what I'd thunk up and he thought I was a pretty smart fellow."

"He could've shot you through the sides," Betty argued.

"Only showed him my front and back."

"Well, he could've shot you in the head."

Tom reached down, picked up and displayed a small frying pan. "Had this in front of my nose all the time. Figgered he wouldn't see it with all the light behind me."

"Stop patting yourself on the back," she continued in vexation. "I still think it was dumb."

"What's going on, Betty?" said, Cora, peering into the porch. "Anybody hurt?'

"We're okay, Cora," Betty replied as she went to and

opened the screen door. "Some stupid thing my husband dreamed up."

"What was all the shooting, Tom?" asked Fred, Cora's husband.

"A fellow's been following me. I thought he was setting a trap for me out on the road today."

"How'd you know he was coming tonight?" another neighbor asked.

"Didn't for sure. I did think it was likely."

To Betty's obvious chagrin, Tom took delight in showing his protection device and explaining his moves in substituting the mannequin in the glider for himself.

"Ain't that a woman's figure?" a neighbor wanted to know.

Tom nodded. "It wasn't one of their best and it was all they was about to loan me. I figgered no one could tell in the dark and a rifle shot away."

George Martinez rode up to the hitching rail, dismounted and stood at the back of the small group.

"Everything's over now, folks," Betty interposed irritably. "Go on with you. Don't give this feeble-headed man of mine any more listening. You come back in the morning, Cora, and help me find some lawyer to put him out to the funny farm."

"Never you mind her, Cora," Tom said. "She's the one who's crazy . . . crazy about me."

As the small gathering of neighbors returned to their homes, Tom motioned for George to come to the porch.

"You had it figgered, Tom," the young man said. He pointed into the darkness. "I was hiding way back up there like you said, but I didn't see him 'til I heard the shots."

"See him afterwards?"

George nodded. "I saw him run for his horse. I jumped on mine and tagged along after him."

"Not too close, did ya?"

"No, he never saw me. I saw where he was going. Took the south road."

"Mexico," Tom said.

"You going after him?"

"Ginger's saddled in the barn."

"Want me to go with you?"

"Nope, you ain't cut out for this."

"What about Judd and his deputy?"

"No law in this town who'd be of any help."

"You got the right to arrest him?" Betty asked.

Tom reached into his shirt pocket and took out a silver badge. "Sheriff Morgan deputized me. Hope it holds up outta his county." He returned the badge to his pocket.

"What can I do?" George asked.

"I'd appreciate if you'd stay here and keep an eye on Betty," Tom answered.

"I still don't like you doing what you did," Betty entered the conversation with her complaint.

"Some day," Tom countered, "he'd pick the time and the place to shoot one or both of us and we'd never know where or when. This way, he thinks I'm dead . . . and now that gives me the edge. I'll go and bring him in one way or another."

"Dead or alive, you're saying?" Betty asked.

Tom shrugged. "I'll give him his choice."

Betty rose and walked to him and embraced him. "I know you're a stubborn man and you'll do this no matter what I say." She paused and looked up into his eyes. "Promise me one thing."

Tom waited.

"No choice, Tom," she said bluntly. "Don't give him no choice at all."

Chapter Thirty-one

Tom rode Ginger at alternate gaits—a few minutes of gallop followed by short times of trotting—as he headed south. He slowed his horse to a walk at the far distant sight of a rider on the road barely visible in the light of the full moon. Gratified at the sight of his presumed quarry, he started the mare forward. He turned Ginger off the road and walked her thirty feet to one side and headed her parallel to the main road. Tom reasoned Jed would glance back for pursuers on the thoroughfare and not for someone following in the mounds, ridges and depressions of the brush land.

He rode over small hillocks, past underbrush and clumps of hardy arid country trees. He relied on his mare's ability to pick a sure path over the rocky ground while he kept his eyes searching ahead to catch an

233

occasional glimpse of the other nighttime rider. *Could be someone else*, Tom considered. *I was so damned sure of myself to Betty. Jed might've gone any other way and I'd be the fool.*

Even so, Tom continued to follow the distant horse-man, reasonably sure it was Jed Porter ahead. He had long considered the strategy of capture. His plan was to trail along unseen until the young man would likely stop to rest his horse and himself from the ride. Riding upon him without warning and taking him by swift sur-prise, the young killer would likely be confused, uncer-tain whether to remount and flee or stand and fight. Either way, Tom felt he would have the advantage.

He rode his mare to the top of a ridge that gave him a high, bright moonlight view of the terrain ahead. The lay of the land in this part of California included rolling hills and bowl-shaped valleys. Also, from place to place in the landscape, immense slabs of granite thrust up through the surface soil—massive stone wedges broken into high mounts of jumbled granite blocks and boul-ders.

Beyond the stretch of relatively level ground, the dark bulk of such a rocky pinnacle rose in the near distance. Once Jed reached that rugged landscape, Tom's advan-tage would lessen. Tom realized he would have to move back onto the road and, possibly, into the fugitive's sight. *Can't wait for him to stop. Best to take him now before he sees me and holes up in them rocks and boulders.*

For an alarming moment, Tom was afraid he had already been seen as the rider spurred his gray horse to a faster pace, but it was a canter not a gallop. If it was Jed Porter, the increase in speed was more likely an indication of the young man's impatient nature than any concern of pursuit.

Tom angled his horse toward the road and, as Ginger came to level ground, Tom leaned forward and spurred her to a gallop in full pursuit. Ahead, the rider appeared not yet aware of the man on horseback gaining on him.

Suddenly, the rider turned in his saddle to look back and, even in the bluish shine of the moon, Tom recognized the silhouette as Jed Porter. With a loud yet unintelligible shout of profanity, Porter whipped his horse into a gallop, spurs digging repeatedly at the animal's sides.

Damn! So much for surprise!

Jed twisted again and Tom saw the flash from the young man's revolver and, barely, heard the report despite the pounding of Ginger's hoofs. Again, there was a flash and the sound of a shot. As yet, no bullet had whirred near him. Tom drew his revolver from his holster although he held no thought of shooting from the jolting ride of a galloping horse. *Let him waste 'em!*

The space separating the racing riders was narrowing although the distance to the rocky sanctuary was lessening as well. Tom, leaning low, his head near Ginger's right ear, spoke to his mare, urging her to lengthen her stride, to strive harder for speed.

No more shots came from Jed as he hunched over the

mane of his galloping steed. He was whipping his horse and heading off the road to the nearest uplift of stone. Fifty yards, forty, thirty and, at last, he pulled his rifle, vaulted down and sprinted the last ten yards to take cover behind a wall of tumbled boulders, his horse slowing and trotting back to the road.

Tom spurred Ginger toward the riderless horse, slowing almost to a stop to lean down and grasp the dangling reins. He gave them a sharp pull and prodded his mare forward, ignoring the bullet that cut with a whirr through the air a foot away. He galloped Ginger and Jed's horse round an intervening rock wall out of Jed's line of fire. Tom swung down from the saddle and tethered both horses to a fir tree. He reached for his own rifle and moved quickly to flatten against the rock wall, edging his way back to where he had last seen Jed. "Jed Porter!" Tom called. "Bad mistake, boy! I got your horse! You'll have to come through me to get back to him!"

"Who the hell are you?" came the shouted reply. "Why are you chasing me?"

"A ghost! Come to haunt ya!"

"Patterson? You can't be!"

"Come look and see. Drop your guns and walk out, hands high!"

"I shot you!"

"You shot a dress shop dummy! Drop your guns and come out!"

"You ruined my life! I'm dead broke and on the run! All because of you, damn you!"

There was a long period of silence.

"You'll have to come after me, I ain't coming out!

"I'll wait!" Tom yelled.

"I ain't gonna hang!"

"Maybe you will or maybe you won't! Maybe you'll do time and, someday, you might even get out!"

There was no response.

Tom realized whatever advantage he had left was not much of one at all. True, he had Jed's horse and eliminated his ride, but he had failed to catch Porter in the open. All he had done was to drive a dangerous man to cover. Many hours remained before sunrise and, even with the full moon, the night painted black shadows into the crevices, fissures and clefts in the rocks. If the young man refused to come out, if he moved higher, circling through the crests and hollows of the mountain's rough landscape, he might very well become the hunter rather than the prey.

"Flush him out, no other way," Tom said in a low voice, shaking his head. "Get him before he goes in deeper." Climbing into that murky maze of rocky pits and shrouded crags would make him a target and the advantage would surely shift to the youthful killer.

As if his thoughts had been read, Tom heard the scrape of boots and the metallic clank of a rifle barrel touching stone. Jed was moving.

Tom bent low and moved to the rounded corner of a boulder. He lay flat on his belly and crawled a few inches forward to get a partial view of the area where

Jed had been hiding. For a minute, perhaps more, he could see nothing in the shadows at ground level. Then, fifteen feet up the craggy slope, he caught a glimpse of Jed darting from the shelter of one huge rock to the refuge of another. Tom realized his own position was in the brightest of the moonlight and he inched back.

A bullet punched into the ground a half-foot from his face, the sound of the shot bouncing from the rocks above.

"Last chance, Jed!" Tom called. "I don't want to kill you but I will. Give it up and come on down."

Another bullet spanked the dirt and the report echoed in the still night.

Tom noted the large expanse of open ground that lay between his position and the first tumble of sizable boulders that would give him cover. Jed could sit in his high position and shoot him over and over even should he dash across that exposed killing ground. Tom rolled to his feet as he retreated, his eyes cast upward, looking for an alternative means of assault.

Twelve feet above, a sizable, chest-high niche in the rock wall appeared to be safe from Jed's aim. Just above it, a sixty-five degree slanting rock face angled toward the top of the mount. Tom stepped back to get a better view; the slope extended to a high ledge, an attack position much better than Jed's. To reach the niche, he looked for and found handholds and narrow ridges for his boot tips.

"Son of a gun," Tom muttered. "Mountain goat again."

Realizing his rifle to be a hindrance in a climb, he stashed it under a nearby bush and returned to the rock wall. He reached his right hand high for the first finger hold in a minute crevice, found an edge for the toe of his left boot and pulled himself three feet up the stony surface. He crabbed his way up the wall with short moves and reached the niche.

To his satisfaction, he was well hidden from Jed's line of fire. The rock incline was a challenge. In the moonlight, he could see no chinks or cracks in the smooth surface. A few small stone protuberances might be helpful, but he would need to scale the slippery gradient using the strength of his arms, legs, hands, and fingers all pressing down to overcome the pull of gravity. He lay facedown and began to slowly crawl his way up the steep rock face.

Two minutes later, he pulled himself prone onto the ledge. He crawled forward and surveyed his surrounding area. He judged he was about four feet higher than Jed's last position, but he swept his eyes across the jagged mount with care. He had made his ascent with as little noise as possible and hoped it had been quiet enough not to reveal his presence. He took note of possible angles of danger and scrunched under a small overhang.

Now, I wait. Tom drew his revolver and covered the hammer with his hand to mute the sound of the click as he cocked it. *Wait 'til he shows himself.*

"You coming after me?" came a shout from behind

crag ten feet across and a few feet down. "You coming up?"

Tom smiled. Jed thought he was still at ground level.

"Answer me, you hear?" Jed said aloud, a complaint uttered in vexation.

Nothing to do but wait, Tom decided in silence.

Fifteen minutes later, Jed emerged from his hiding place, crouching low and climbing up the slope, the rifle in his right hand, using his left to touch the stone slant for balance as he moved into Tom's full view.

"You're dead in my sights, boy," Tom said in a strong, calm voice. "I won't miss."

Jed froze and let out a sigh.

"Drop the rifle," Tom said. "Don't even think of trying anything."

Jed sighed again and dropped the rifle, glancing back as it skittered on the rocky surface and slid a few feet down and out of sight.

"Keep that one hand on the ground and unbuckle that gun belt with the other. Don't reach for that hogleg."

"Okay, but don't shoot," the young man said, his hand moving very slowly, very deliberately toward the belt buckle. "I'm giving myself up." He started to rise.

"Stay down!" Tom barked.

The young man looked bewildered, his face showing fear. "I'm sorry," he whimpered. "I didn't mean—"

Suddenly, he dove down the slope, a suicidal leap. Tom's belated shot ticked at Jed's hip bringing a yelp of pain as the young man hit and rolled out of sight with Tom's gunfire chasing.

"Getting old and stupid, Tom," he scolded himself. He reloaded his Peacemaker and inched forward to see if he could get a look, not knowing what he would see.

"I ain't dead, Tom!" Jed called, nowhere in sight.

"Well, that's my mistake. I ain't gonna make another."

"Looks like I got you treed now."

Tom nodded in silent agreement. *He can get to the horses before me.*

He scooted back to the slope and pushed off on his back, feet first. It was a wild slide of twenty feet that would surely catapult him in a fall to the hard surface of the road from a height that would stun and disable if it didn't cripple him.

At the last possible moment, he spread his arms and jammed his boot heels against the stone surface, the granite tearing at his jacket sleeves as he bounced along and only slightly slowed his skidding descent. His momentum plunged him feet first into the niche where one boot touched its base for only a scant pause in his flight and then he arced out to the roadside below trying to flex his knees as he hit and rolled. The breath knocked from him, sore and battered, he tried to rise, and then fell back.

"I'll be back for you, Patterson! You and your missus." Jed was shouting up at the slope as he ran limping into sight, then whirled and stopped as he caught sight of Tom's crumpled figure in the bright moonlight.

Tom reached to his holster for his revolver. *Not*

there! Then, he saw it ten feet away, only a stride away from Jed's feet.

Jed saw it too.

"Well, well," young Porter said, sauntering forward. He paused and leaned down to pick up the handgun. "Looks like you had yourself quite a fall there, Mr. Tom." He walked forward, watching the defenseless man closely and aiming the revolver.

"Think I broke a rib," Tom said, his hand at his side.

"I'll just have to put you out of your misery," Jed said and pointed the barrel of Tom's revolver at his chest. "Your own gun, don't you wish you had it 'stead of me?"

"This'll do," Tom replied as his hand brought out the pepperbox and fired.

Jed blinked his astonishment and looked down at the dark spot blossoming on his shirt. He tried to re-aim the revolver, but Tom's second shot hit him just below the throat and Jed fell backward onto the roadside, his dying eyes staring into the smiling face of the approving moon.

Chapter Thirty-two

The following morning, Tom lay soaking in a tub of warm water in the kitchen, his eyes closed, feeling the heat soothing his aches. His eyelids opened at the sound of Betty's approach and watched as, near his feet, she added a small trickle of boiling water from a steaming pail.

"Paddle it around some," she instructed. "Mix it in so I don't cook your feet off."

"This ought to do it," he said, reaching his hands to scoop the hot water back toward him. "Couple of more minutes and I'll get out."

"Still sore?" Betty asked.

"Getting better. Two baths in two days, that's a record."

Betty walked across to the back door and poured out

the rest of the water. Then, she pulled a chair from the kitchen table and placed it near the tub and sat down.

"Hey, I'm taking a bath here," Tom complained.

"So?"

"Well, you ain't gonna just sit and stare, are you?"

"Why, 'cause you're naked?"

"Well . . . yes."

She laughed. "You were naked when I was pouring water a minute ago."

"That's different."

She chuckled, then sobered. "Are we done with all the shooting and serving the law and whatever?"

Uncomfortable under her gaze, Tom rubbed the soap bar in his hands and spread the lather on the surface of the bathwater. "I 'spect so. Bad folks are all dead or in jail now."

"Good," she said with an approving nod. "Think you could be a regular sort of fellow, settle down, stay home and mind your own business?"

"Yeah, I guess."

"Good," she repeated. "How'd you like to be a father?"

Tom stared at her, his nakedness forgotten. "Why . . . I didn't think you could—"

"Not me, you're right about that," she interrupted. She took a folded sheet of paper from her apron and opened it. "I got a letter awhile back from Joe Calvecci while you was galavanting around. You remember Miss Pauline back at the Gold Strike in Colorado?"

Tom nodded.

"After he sold the saloon, Joe opened another down there in Texas. Pauline went with him and then . . . she was always peaked . . . she died of consumption down there in Dallas. She had a little boy, almost three now."

"That's sad news. Pauline was always a friendly girl."

"She was a good sort."

"Boy's pa going to take him?"

Betty shook her head. "He took off for parts unknown."

They sat in silence for almost a minute.

"That's the letter from Joe?"

"He didn't know who else."

"For us to take the boy?"

She nodded.

"Humph," Tom grunted and paddled his feet in the water for a few moments. "A boy, huh? Well, maybe that'd be okay. Might be just fine. You and me, we'll give it some thinking."

"After we got back from Placerville, when everything looked settled, I wrote to Joe and, well . . ."

Tom studied her as he slowly ran a soapy washcloth over his left shoulder. "Already made up *our* minds, did you?"

She gave a shy smile. "Is that okay with you? You don't mind?"

He grinned. "We're getting a little long in the tooth to be parents, but sure, that's fine, just fine. Be nice to have a young 'un around the place. I think I'd like that."

"Then wash up and get dressed. We've got to hurry."

He cocked his head, a questioning pose.

She reached into her apron pocket again and brought out a folded telegram. "This here is a wire from Joe. Came here yesterday, but with all that was going on . . ." She paused. "He's bringing the kid on the train to Auburn."

"How soon?"

"Real soon."

"Like . . . when?"

"Like . . . on the afternoon train . . . today."

"Today?" Tom sat up, splashing water out of the tub. "You mean, *today*?"

"Oh, and one more thing while we're there. You remember taking some of the Wilsons' things to Auburn where they were fixing to live?"

"How could I forget?" Tom snorted. "All them folks snickering when we unloaded that outhouse."

"The Wilsons decided not to move there after all. We'll be needing to bring what things they sent over back home again."

"Lordy, Bett!"

She giggled.

A Negro, conservatively dressed in a dark blue suit, celluloid collar and colorful cravat, came out of the parlor car onto the rear platform of the train. With a nod to a dapper, white-haired gentleman at the railing, he watched the town of Auburn diminish in sight as the train gathered speed.

"Afternoon," the dapper gentleman said. "Going to Sacramento?"

"On past," the Negro replied. "San Francisco."

"Joseph Calvecci." He extended his hand.

"Isaiah Washington. They call me Ike," the Negro said as they shook hands.

"I'm heading to 'Frisco myself," Calvecci said. "Looking to setting up a new enterprise." He cocked his head to indicate the surrounding countryside. "You from around here?"

"Down around Placerville. Had some business in the Comstock and caught the train up at Reno." He paused. "Saw you and a little tyke get off and visit with some folks. Know them well?"

Calvecci nodded. "Quite well. I brought the boy out from Dallas. His mother, a widow and one of my employees, passed away. Tom Patterson and his fine wife, both good friends of myself and the deceased, they've agreed to raise the boy as their own."

"That was very nice of them." Ike paused. "It just so happens, I met that Patterson man some time back. Seems like then, he was in some kind of trouble."

Calvecci chuckled. "That would be Tom. He's a lucky fellow. He gets into trouble, but he does have a knack for getting clear each and every time. He's fine, now."

"That's good to hear. I liked him."

"How'd you come to meet Tom?"

"I did some prospecting down there in the hills," Ike said. "I guess you could call it a chance meeting . . .

during that time he was getting himself clear. We spent some time together."

Calvecci gave a smile. "Possible you might've had a hand in helping out?"

"Maybe. You say Mr. Tom is lucky. Maybe that sort of luck kinda rubs off." He paused and gazed at the snowcaps on the distant Sierra Nevada peaks. "After meeting the man and, in a way of helping him out, I gave him the loan of my mule. Now, I've been prospecting on and off for five or six years now. Never found more than a few little nuggets. Coming back with Buster, that's my mule, we came a different direction than I'd ever been before. Sun was coming up and, all of a sudden, I caught this sight of gold sparkling out of a gully."

"Good strike?" Calvecci asked.

Ike nodded. "Pure luck. More than enough to buy me a nice place to live for the rest of my life way up high on a hill looking down at the San Francisco bay."

"Traveling alone?"

Ike nodded.

"Me too. Can I buy you a drink?"

"A toast to the Patterson family, if they'll allow a colored man."

"Let's see what money can do."

Calvecci turned and ushered Isaiah through the door.